He Pulled Her Into His Arms And Covered Her Mouth With His.

"You sure know how to get a man's day started."

Lindsey's breath caught as she panted softly. "Marco, I never meant for this to happen. You've got to believe me. We can't—"

"We just did."

"But you hardly know me."

"I know what I feel, and I've got a damned good idea about what you feel, too."

"What we feel doesn't have anything to do with it. We can't do this."

"Kiss? Enjoy each other's company? If either one of us had fewer professional ethics, we'd be making love right this minute, up against those file cabinets or underneath my drawing board."

Dear Reader,

Readers ask me what *I* think Silhouette Desire is. To me, Desire love stories are sexy, sassy, emotional and dynamic books about the power of love.

I demand variety, and strive to bring you six unique stories each month. These stories might be quite different, but each promises a wonderful love story with a happy ending.

This month, there's something I know you've all been waiting for: the next installment in Joan Hohl's *Big, Bad Wolfe* series, July's *Man of the Month, Wolfe Watching*. Here, undercover cop Eric Wolfe falls hard for a woman who is under suspicion.... Look for more *Big, Bad Wolfe* stories later in 1994.

As for the rest of July, well, things just keep getting hotter, starting with *Nevada Drifter,* a steamy ranch story from Jackie Merritt. And if you like your Desire books fun and sparkling, don't miss Peggy Moreland's delightful *The Baby Doctor*.

As all you "L.A. Law" fans know, there's nothing like a good courtroom drama (I *love* them myself!), so don't miss Doreen Owens Malek's powerful, gripping love story *Above the Law*. Of course, if you'd rather read about single moms trying to get single guys to love them—*and* their kids—don't miss Leslie Davis Guccione's *Major Distractions*.

To complete July we've found a tender, emotional story from a wonderful writer, Modean Moon. The book is titled *The Giving,* and it's a bit different for Silhouette Desire, so please let me know what you think about this very special love story.

So there you have it: drama, romance, humor and suspense, all rolled into six books in one fabulous line—Silhouette Desire. Don't miss any of them.

All the best,

Lucia Macro
Senior Editor

Please address questions and book requests to:
Silhouette Reader Service
U.S.: 3010 Walden Ave., P.O. Box 1325, Buffalo, NY 14269
Canadian: P.O. Box 609, Fort Erie, Ont. L2A 5X3

LESLIE DAVIS GUCCIONE
MAJOR DISTRACTIONS

SILHOUETTE *Desire*®
Published by Silhouette Books
America's Publisher of Contemporary Romance

SILHOUETTE BOOKS

ISBN 0-373-05870-5

MAJOR DISTRACTIONS

LESLIE DAVIS GUCCIONE

now writes from Pittsburgh, Pennsylvania. After twenty years in rural Duxbury, Massachusetts, she and her family are enjoying city life. When not plotting romances, Leslie is the award-winning author of books for middle grade and young adult readers.

For Gail

One

"You can't be! That bad . . . ? No, of course not, go back to bed. Really, I'll be fine. . . . I'll think of something. You know me, the survivor." Lindsey Major wiped a smudge of clown white off the receiver and placed the phone in its cradle.

"No matter what I try, fate's got a custard pie up its sleeve," she muttered.

She pushed her purple curls back in place and glared at the fuchsia ruffles around her wrists as she drummed her fingers on an unopened carton. Through the office door of Three Wishes she could see that the grand opening was well underway. Parents and their excited children were perusing the boutique shelves, which brimmed with books, clever educational games and handcrafted toys. The shop was tucked into half of what had originally been the bucolic train station of Dorset Mills, Delaware, a quaint, mansard-roofed building that also housed the post office. It had been Lindsey's first mailing address as a bride.

Dorset Mills was a country crossroads in the hills separating Wilmington from the Brandywine Valley, a lush area punctuated by estates and a few private roads. The grist mills of the Dorset family had once ground grain to flour on the banks of the Brandywine River, as had hundreds of others.

Dorset Court was a riverside expanse of fieldstone mill houses, converted in the 1940s to exclusive co-operative apartments and condominiums. It was an address with a waiting list. The units rarely came on the market; they were usually sold privately or handed down from parent to child. Jonathan Russell's name had been on the list for two years when Lindsey married him. When they'd separated the spring before last, the same connections had landed him a smaller, but equally prestigious unit overlooking the game preserve that bordered the property. He'd lived there until his death.

Her memories were still painful, compounded now by professional problems. "I should have known it would be a bad omen," she muttered as she glanced through the window. The slate roofs of the exclusive address were just visible from the north. She turned and cleared her mind of the unpleasant reverie. "The show must go on." She drummed her fingers on her thigh as she tried to devise an alternate plan. The show *would* go on, just as her life had. She'd think of something.

For the occasion, bunting draped the front of the building. The wide, wooden platform was to be used for Lindsey's performance. The gravel parking lot had been turned into a picnic spot with tables and refreshments, and families anxious for the entertainment dotted the area.

Lindsey could see Anne Beckford, Three Wishes's owner, smiling for a photographer and checking her watch. She began to chat anxiously with a man in a flamboyant shirt, who seemed to be peppering her with questions. The press. Lindsey groaned at her circumstances. Amanda Mendenhall, the owner of the firm that had hired her as entertainment, had mentioned that she would also alert the Wilmington paper.

The reporter was what her college friends would have called worth-a-second-look handsome, in a confident, offbeat sort of way. From what she could tell through the panes of the window, he seemed less than enthusiastic about his assignment.

Unobserved, Lindsey gave herself the luxury of a few stolen glances. The man *was* worth a second look. Since that was all she intended to allow herself, she indulged in a moment of anonymous appreciation. Dark hair, dark eyes, perhaps a flamboyant disposition to match his shirt, or maybe a conventional one to complement his traditional khaki trousers and loafers. If clothes made the man, this one could be just about anything.

He finally stepped from view and reality returned. Lindsey forced herself to concentrate on her circumstances. Her enormous chartreuse sneakers made pacing impossible. Instead, she continued to tap out an anxious rhythm with her polka-dotted fingernails, pausing long enough to apply her bulbous, lavender latex nose as she searched her brain for an alternate plan.

"Lindsey Major?"

She turned around. The reporter was now smiling at her from the doorway, hands in his pockets, head cocked to one side. His dark hair was thick and unruly, his eyebrows arched inquisitively. He rocked back on his heels and looked her over, head to toe, as if he were aware that she'd just done the same thing to him. Lindsey played with her neck ruffles. Suddenly he grinned broadly, which animated his face, deepened his complexion and put her entirely on the defensive.

He laughed as he looked at her, then murmured, "Forgive me."

"I'd have to forgive you if you *didn't* laugh," she replied. Handsome as he was, what held Lindsey's attention was his shirt. At close range, the flamboyant print proved to be a wild Hawaiian design of tropical fronds and exotic plants. The pattern billowed over his chest in a dozen shades, from red to vermilion and lavender, the ideal complement to the colors of her clown suit, nose, wig and nails. She sized him up as a broad-shouldered five foot ten or eleven, a journalist with a sense of style. She sent up a silent prayer that he also had a sense of humor. The solution to her problem was about to shake her hand.

"I'm Marco D'Abruzzi." He chuckled. "That's quite a creative getup."

"Kids like the unexpected. No red nose for this clown." Lindsey pushed a button in her cuff and a smiley face on her hugely padded bottom began to blink frantically. Marco shook his head, then yanked his hand back. "Is there a buzzer in that palm of yours?"

She wiggled her dotted fingernails. "One can never be too sure. You'll just have to trust me."

"Implicitly." Marco's bemused expression swept over her again. This time when he put out his hand, he stepped forward. His eyes were hickory, softened by equally dark, thick lashes and frank curiosity. Lindsey took his hand, held it, caught the look of surprise and waited.

He glanced at his palm and found a stick of gum. "Very good! What other tricks do you perform?"

"I'm not a magician. I work with puppets and stories."

"There's quite a gathering out there. You must be about ready to go on."

"Not quite." She swallowed, made a snap judgment and followed her instinct. "What would it take to persuade you to weave a little fantasy with me?"

"Am I being propositioned by a clown?"

"Yes, as a matter of fact. I'm desperate."

"So much for my appeal."

Lindsey stepped closer and calmed her nerves, hoping she sounded a lot more confident than she felt. "I've got one major problem. My partner just called in sick. Food poisoning. I need her more as a prop than anything else." She put her fingers to his shirt, stopping just short of touching it. "As you can see, between your shirt and my costume, the purples and reds are perfectly matched. We're color coordinated already.''

He took a step backward. "Oh, no, you don't.''

She brazenly fluffed the hair at his temple. "I'll bet a little water will bring out some fabulous curls. I wish they were lavender, but brown hair will do. You can wear my sneakers. The toes are just stuffed with newspaper.'' This time she poked his chest. He seemed astounded.

"No. Really. I'm sorry your partner's sick, but I'm no clown. I'm sure you'll think of something—or someone—else.''

"There isn't time.'' Desperation and the anonymity of full makeup and costume gave her audacity she didn't know she possessed. She held his arm and wished she could remember what he'd said his last name was. "Mr...Marco, I'm a puppeteer, but rather than a stage, I use another clown as my prop. I can ad-lib most of what Betsy would have done. All I need is your body.''

"My body.''

"Your body. I've got all the dialogue, all the moves.''

"I won't argue with that.''

"Don't make me blush or all this gooey makeup'll run.''

"After this performance, I can't imagine that blushing is part of your repertoire. I'd like to help, really, but I've got another appointment at four o'clock. Besides, I'm no good with kids. I don't know anything about entertaining children.'' He glanced at the window. "And there are dozens of the terrifying little rug rats out there."

Lindsey lowered her head and stared at her feet as she flapped her sneakers. "All waiting to have their innocent, trusting hearts broken by the mean clown who didn't show up."

Marco laughed. "First you flirt, now you lay on the guilt."

"I was not flirting!"

"There was a plea for my body."

"I need a prop, that's all."

"Use one of the kids as a prop."

"Too common. Spoils the effect."

"You're very good at persuasion."

"Not good enough, apparently."

He chuckled again. "You're breaking my heart, but I can't help you, really. This appointment—"

"We'll be finished before four, I promise." Lindsey batted her inch-long false eyelashes and stared—hard—into his eyes. His astonishment had turned to amusement, but he didn't look convinced. "I really need this to be perfect."

"I'm not a performer."

"I'm not either, most of the time." She tried to sound serious, fully aware of how ridiculous she looked. "I'm a free-lance copywriter—advertising, public relations, brochures. I've been hired by Mendenhall and Lipton to do this show. I've been trying for months to get my foot in the door with the owner. She's tough to work for, but her accounts are strong and she pays well. Her agency's one of the best. I do this puppeteering on the side, but my bread and butter is writing. If I foul this up, I won't have a prayer at real work.''

"She can make or break your reputation?''

"Free-lancing depends on references and track records. Let's just say that my financial well-being could be greatly enhanced by Amanda Mendenhall.'' She took his arm again, hoping the seriousness in her voice counterbalanced her appearance. ''I was supposed to see her next week for a writing assignment, but she's gone for a month on a combined business-honeymoon trip. She suddenly up and remarried her ex-husband.''

"I know.''

"She left before giving me the work, or seeing me perform, unfortunately. Don't you see, you could help salvage this performance. Anne Beckford will tell her I was worth the expense. I realize this all sounds ridiculous and it's not your normal sort of request. Believe me, I'm not used to begging perfect strangers to act like clowns. It's just that I'm desperate. A little,'' she added as she waved her hand in the air, embarrassed at the sudden seriousness of her tone and the edge of panic in her voice.

"You aren't going to get all weepy on me, are you?''

"Weepy? Of course not.''

"If blushing makes your makeup gooey, I can imagine what tears would do. Probably unglue those eyelashes, for starters.''

"I'm not weepy, Mr. DeLuca.''

"D'Abruzzi.''

"Whatever.''

"Marco D'Abruzzi. Under the circumstances, you'd do well to remember it.''

Two

"Now, your best he-man pose." Lindsey Major's husky whisper had a Southern lilt to it. This time it was at his right ear, and it once again played havoc with Marco's nervous system. As the audience in front of them laughed and clapped, Marco sucked in a breath, swelled his chest and opened his hands at his waist.

Checking on a writer-puppeteer's performance was the last thing he'd wanted on his weekend agenda. He had a tennis date at four and a backlog of design work after that. Suddenly a sock-puppet lamb danced over his right shoulder, breaking his train of thought. Next a sock-puppet puppy inched its way around his ribs in search of the *baa, baa, baa* Lindsey was gently bleating at his ear. He could feel her breath on his jaw. His skin alternated between gooseflesh and hot flashes. The shock made him stand perfectly still.

As she narrated her outlandish story, the lamb danced over his natural curls. Curls! As usual, that morning he'd spent an inordinate amount of time getting rid of them, only to have Lindsey Major's polka-dotted fingertips massage them into a froth with some sprinkles of tap water.

"Not as terrific as my purple wig, but you'll do," she'd said. His scalp had tingled through the entire episode.

By the time she'd finished applying the clown makeup to his face, he was unable to trust his voice. His head prickled with sensations from crown to chin. Now, as the youngsters cheered the puppy bounding across his chest, ill-timed and unwarranted pleasure coursed through his body. Lindsey's clown touch was everywhere at once, then nowhere, leaving a trail of sensations that soothed and irritated simultaneously. Thirty families were seated in front of him watching her antics, and he sent a thank-you heavenward as a stiff spring breeze caught the sleeves of his shirt and offered relief.

"Take a deep bow," came the voice at his left ear.

He bent over, and the puppeteer finger-walked her creations lightly up his spine into his hair. From belt to collar, the pleasure teased. He stayed bent at the waist as the clown took off the puppets and leaned over to match his bow. Her bare feet peeked out from beneath the droopy lace of her billowing pantaloons. He glimpsed purple toenail polish. Impulsively he took her hand and grinned at the audience, aware that she'd turned to stare at him, those blue eyes wide under the false fringe of her lashes.

With every cheer from the audience, they bowed together. Each time, her fingers wound tighter with his.

"They loved us," he whispered. The look came again, and as the audience began to disperse, she turned for the store.

In Lindsey's oversize sneakers, Marco clomped after her into the shop. He had half a mind to take her hand again and keep going, into the parking lot, out into the sunset, anywhere they could be alone and she could keep right on working her magic. She'd said she was no magician, but Lindsey Major, whoever she might be under all the ruffles and makeup, gave new meaning to the word *fantasy*. Marco D'Abruzzi was not at all adverse to being the object of hers.

"You're a natural," she was saying as they reached the office.

He closed the door after them. "You have a way with puppets that has to be seen to be believed, or in my case, felt."

"Kids love the chase."

Kids. "I can name a few adults who enjoyed it, too." He balanced on the edge of the desk. "You got me into this goop—I hope you know how to get it off."

"A little more difficult, but not much." She handed him a box of tissues and tucked a towel into his open shirt. He closed his eyes. With one hand she held his bangs off his face and with the other began to wipe off the clown white. In the privacy of the small space, the pleasure returned, small coils of heat spiraling much lower than his jaw, where Lindsey now ran the tissue. More than once he could have sworn that her hand trembled.

She cleared her throat. "I wish Amanda Mendenhall had been here. She's so demanding, and this might have warmed her up a little."

"You are good at warming up a person."

Lindsey suddenly stopped. Her hand *was* trembling. The silence grew awkward as she stared at the tissue. After another swipe with it, she wiped her hands. "Marco, I think you should finish this yourself."

Their eyes met, and he was entranced by the depth in hers. The contrast of the clown white and the thick, fake lashes made them seem nearly aquamarine, deep as a pool as she blinked. She handed him a jar of petroleum jelly. "You can get the rest off with this and some soap and water in the bathroom over there."

If Lindsey Major were playing a game with rules of her own, this was no time to call her hand. He let the moment pass and put the jar on the desk.

Suddenly she touched his arm again. "Marco, I'm sorry. Where's my head? I never should have said anything like that."

"Anything like what?" he replied as he tried to recall which remark she might be regretting. The double entendre, the *entre nous* tone in her voice and the intimacy in her touch were languages all their own.

"What I said about Amanda Mendenhall was off the record."

"Business?" He forced himself to clear his head. "Fine."

"What's your four o'clock assignment?"

"Tennis."

"You cover sports, as well?"

"Sports? No, I have a weekly game." Lindsey Major astounded him. She was nothing but a conglomeration of lavender and purples, clown paint, billowing pantaloons and scampering sock puppets. He didn't know her face or figure, wouldn't recognize her out of costume if she were in the same room. The pleasure of her touch bordered on the erotic. He was convinced that she knew it.

"Do you have a business card?" he asked, to continue the conversation.

"For business?"

"Did you have something else in mind?"

"Of course not."

Once again he was taken aback, agitated all the more by his inability to see her face and read her expression. It made him feel uncustomarily transparent, adolescent. He glanced at her ring finger, aware that the lack of rings could have easily been due to the performance, rather than marital status, but surely... The woman had a style that threatened to melt what was left of his reserve. Her banter challenged him; her determination impressed him.

"Good luck with your writing," he managed to say

as she fished a card from her purse and handed it to him. He stood up to leave.

"Thanks." Her reply was soft. Beneath her thick mink eyelashes, her blue eyes flashed again. It was all he knew of her.

They both paused. "Lindsey, there's been some misunderstanding."

"I hope you haven't mistaken my... persuasion... for something else. This is very awkward."

"That can wait. I should explain something first."

They turned at the sound of a knock and the opening of the door. "Ms. Major? I'm Sarah Brant from the *Morning News*. We've got some good shots. I wonder if you've got time for a quick interview?"

Marco's heart thumped from pure guilt and the lousy timing. He grimaced as the clown paused and turned from the reporter back to him.

"I don't understand. I've already given an interview," Lindsey said.

Marco shrugged sheepishly. "I was just about to explain all that. I'm the creative director for Mendenhall and Lipton. I'd love the chance to straighten this out over dinner, after my four o'clock appointment."

"Creative director for Amanda Mendenhall?"

"Yes."

"And you let me go on and on. You never explained."

"I tried. How about tonight?"

"Of course not!"

He glanced at his watch. "Then the best I can do is swamp you with apologies in the morning. Stop by the office for your check. I'll explain everything. Nine-thirty?" Before the wide-eyed, lavender-nosed clown could protest, he left for his appointment.

Three

———

"**Y**ou won't forget? Baseball practice at three-thirty?"

Lindsey kissed her eight-year-old. "Lexie, I'll be here when you get home from school."

"I'm Alex now, Mom. Can't you remember? No more baby names."

"You're Alexandra Major Russell to me, darling, no matter what nickname you come up with."

"I choose Alex for baseball, just like you choose Major for work."

"Fair enough. I'll try to remember."

It had been a conscious choice to use her maiden name professionally. Lindsey Major, writer, publicist was easy to find in the phone book and advertising directories. Lindsey Russell, single mother of three, lead a separate, private existence.

At the familiar sound of the approaching school bus, Lindsey turned to her six-year-old twins. "Pucker up, you two, your chariot's arriving."

"What'd you make me for lunch?" Brooke asked as she kissed her mother.

"A chocolate-and-fluff sandwich with jelly-bean salad."

Her twin scoffed. "Right. That means it's really sprouts or ham or something else gross. Why's everything have to be good for us? Andy Stern's mother puts real sodas in his lunch and the biggest snack cakes you ever saw."

Lindsey planted the final kiss on her son. "Justin, I'm your mom, not Andrew's."

"Come on, you guys," Lexie said. "If you two would buy lunch tickets like normal kids, you wouldn't have to put up with Mom's yukky sandwiches."

The squeak of the bus brakes and the whine of the opening door halted the conversation. Lindsey stood on the front walk long enough to see the three of them aboard before locking the house and changing mental gears.

On the ride into Wilmington she would have preferred to think about the twins' upcoming science project or Lexie's—Alex's—batting average. Instead she fumed about Marco whatever-his-name-was. Since yesterday afternoon, she'd thought of little else.

He'd let her go on about Amanda; he'd let her ramble about her need for employment, her desire to make a good impression. Lindsey gritted her teeth.

Recalling the last five minutes of her encounter with him made her furious, a fury mixed with humiliation.

Nevertheless, Marco was also the stranger who had appeared in her makeshift dressing room, agreed to her half-baked bailout scheme, let her dress him in clown makeup and make a spectacle of him in front of throngs of children and their parents. He deserved credit for being a good sport. If only he hadn't made a pass at her, then pretended to be a reporter. Of course, she had to admit it hadn't actually been a pass, but there was no doubt it would have been if she'd let things go any further.

That brought her right back to the emotion that had drawn her to him in the first place—the small flutter, the pulse jump when she'd spied him through the office window. She couldn't blame Marco for that, not when it emanated from her own respiratory system.

She associated those feelings with Marco as much as the fury, and those were ones she tried to bury the moment they cropped up on the edge of her consciousness. She was not a flirt. She doubted if she could remember how. At this stage of her life, there was no point to it. At this stage of her life, there was no time.

She'd been nearly derailed by romance. Now three children depended body and soul on her levelheaded business sense and ability. Some curly haired, Hawaiian-shirted clown's assistant was not going to get her off the track. Especially one who was about to hand her a paycheck.

Lindsey was still mulling over her situation as she drove through the traffic in Rodney Square and around the corner to Stowman Place. There were pieces missing from this Marco puzzle, pieces she would have liked to dismiss, except that the memory of the man himself refused to go away. She'd had no business finger-walking her puppets over him, as if he were some inanimate object. Across his chest, over those shoulders, around his ribs...what could she have been thinking?

She hadn't been thinking. That was the problem. She'd been so bent on pulling off a perfect perform-ance, she'd forgotten propriety. She should have taken his suggestion and improvised with children from the audience. What had she thought she was doing, run-ning her hands through his hair, fluffing curls as if she were giving a scalp massage, applying clown white as if it were a facial and afterward wiping it off his cheeks as if he were one of her children with a grape-juice mustache? Could she blame the man for misunder-standing her intentions?

Lindsey eased her car down the alley to the private lot behind the handsome brick building that housed Mendenhall and Lipton. There was something unde-niably flirtatious about Marco Whomever, about his unabashed cooperation, about the unmistakable look in his eye through all of it—something that for more hours than she cared to admit had kept Lindsey un-able to concentrate on much of anything else.

Flirtatious men came in all sizes and shapes. What gave her pause was that this time she'd enjoyed it. This time the pumping adrenaline, the racing pulse had been hers.

"Straighten up," she muttered as she parked her car.

She locked the door and checked her watch. She had just enough time to pick up her check from M & L and then scoot up the street to the First Trust building, where she was due to hand in the rough copy for *Bravo*, the monthly newsletter she wrote for the Brandywine Valley Opera Company. Having the second appointment cushioned her resolve. She'd stay with Marco only as long as was necessary.

The agency of Mendenhall and Lipton was small, relatively new in the area and rumored to be free of the inflated egos the industry was famous for. Although Lindsey had been in the offices only once, to discuss the puppet show and future writing assignments, the air of warmth and intimacy was unmistakable. As a free-lancer, she tolerated the vagaries of account executives in her continuing search for well-paying assignments. That often meant accepting work she didn't care for, from men she liked even less.

From what she could tell, M & L, as it was known in the business, was a breath of fresh air. Amanda Mendenhall had hinted that she had more work than M & L could handle in-house. Lindsey had intended to convince the tough-but-fair agency president that she was their answer. She was less than comfortable with the assumption that in Amanda's absence, Marco was the one she'd be convincing.

Karen Winters, the receptionist, sat at a desk in the foyer with small offices opening around her. She appeared to remember Lindsey as she gave her name. "I was to see Marco and pick up my check."

"Right, the opening of Three Wishes. I hear you had the kids spellbound."

"Really? Thanks."

Karen laughed. "Of course, your able assistant is taking all the credit. I don't know how you talked him into it, but I wish I'd seen him in action. Clown costumes are about all that awful Hawaiian shirt is good for."

Lindsey lowered her voice. "What the heck is his last name?"

"D'Abruzzi. Two z's." She spelled it. "You don't have to whisper. He's gone to get his excuse for breakfast at the corner deli. He'll be right back. You can wait in his office."

Marco sipped his scalding coffee as he entered the M & L town house. The enticing aroma from the warm muffins he was carrying made his mouth water, although the thought of another rushed meal at his drawing board sent a fresh wave of frustration to mingle with the adrenaline that kept him going. "Overworked and underpaid," he muttered as he approached Karen's desk.

"Save it for a sympathetic ear," she quipped. "You have a visitor."

"A client? Not Patrowski. I told him the roughs for the brochure wouldn't be ready until three o'clock."

"It's not Jack Patrowski."

"Then who?"

Karen arched an eyebrow.

"If that gesture's meant to be a comment on my private life, you're on the wrong track. I've done everything but haul in a sleeping bag since Amanda took off.''

He stepped sideways and glanced across the foyer into his office. A blonde was standing at his drawing board, stretching over it for a closer look at the array of sketches, roughs and samples pinned to the bulletin board above it. Her short, fashionable haircut fell around her ears. A pink, open-necked cotton blouse draped softly over curves he would have lingered over had Karen not been glaring at him. Her skirt was straight, slit at the back of the knee. She had on flat shoes, and as she went up on tiptoe, he followed the contours of her calves and enjoyed the welcome pumping in his chest.

"Stop acting like you're in an art gallery, or worse," Karen muttered.

Marco grinned. "I'm just trying to place her. I'm worn out by this job, but I'd remember if someone like that were part of my private life."

"You're slipping, D'Abruzzi."

He glanced at his watch. "That can't be Lindsey Major," he whispered.

Karen grinned, took a pencil from behind her ear and pointed it toward his office. "The puppeteer herself. Why don't you donate that Hawaiian shirt to her costume collection while she's here?"

"My clothes are my soul," he replied as he tapped his green-and-yellow cotton pullover, silk-screened in a banana-fronds print. He headed for his drawing board and got as far as his doorway when his visitor turned. She would have been even more appealing if she'd been smiling. He held out the bag. "Well, hi there. Pull up a stool. Blueberry or oat bran?"

Lindsey looked from his shirt to the cluttered credenza, to the chair piled with paper samples. "I have another appointment. Nothing, thank you."

"Except your check."

"My check, and a few explanations."

He studied her expression, which took fortitude now that she was staring back without a disguise. Her glance was that same unwavering blue, but now those expressive eyes shone from a face devoid of anything but mascara. From the set of her mouth and the way he'd left her the afternoon before, he suspected the flush in her cheeks was natural.

"Things did sort of roll right along yesterday, didn't they?"

"I never would have asked you to help me if I'd known who you were."

"Why not?"

"And I certainly wouldn't have confessed so unprofessionally."

"It wasn't much of a confession."

"I blame myself, but you should have told me who you were. You've put me in a very awkward position."

Marco forced himself to concentrate on what she was saying, and not on the pleasure of putting the woman standing in front of him together with the voice and hands of the clown who had reduced him to five feet eleven inches of raw nerve endings. "I did try. Before I knew it, you were going on about Amanda. I tried to interrupt, but the moment passed. Once you'd blurted out your feelings, you would have been terribly embarrassed if I'd told you who I was. It would have made you a nervous wreck, and you had a show to do."

"That's your explanation?"

"If the situation had been reversed, you would have done the same thing."

"And lead you on? I doubt it."

"You can't accuse me of leading. The minute I walked into that office, you set your sights on me."

"I was desperate."

"Okay, desperately persuasive."

Her composure faltered. "You make it sound as though you're completely innocent. You let me think—"

"You thought what you wanted. There's no harm done. You found a prop, and your show was a hit. I saved the day. Makes me a hero and you a success."

"Forgive me if I don't put you in the hero category. There was more and you know it."

"A healthy amount of flirting, too."

"Just a minute!"

"Don't apologize. You needed help in a hurry. Your ploy worked. It was all very flattering. You're very good."

Her eyes flashed, but she fought a smile. "Don't you dare turn this around."

"In case you have to share some of the blame?"

"Is it possible for me to just pick up my check and get out of here without complete psychoanalysis?"

"I'll settle for a little old-fashioned honesty. There's no harm in my knowing you're anxious to work for us.

There's certainly no problem with my knowing that when you want something badly enough, you'll go to extraordinary ends to accomplish it.''

Four

―

Marco moved a stack of paper samples from his stool and slid it over to Lindsey. When she finally sat down, he took one of her hands and grinned at her surprise. "No more purple polka-dotted nails."

"No more lots of things."

"Do I detect a little Southern accent?"

"You're changing the subject, and getting personal besides."

"You've fluffed my hair and finger-walked over seventy percent of my body. That qualifies me to get personal." He waited for her flush to deepen.

She stared right back at him. "The hair fluffing and finger-walking were sacrifices for financial security."

"It was a standard question. I always ask clowns about their accents. Virginia? North Carolina?"

"Mr. D'Abrusso—"

"D'Abruzzi. Two *z*'s. Marco is fine."

"Whatever." She stopped, as if the repartee and resolve were suddenly too much effort. "Raleigh, North Carolina. That has nothing to do with the situation. I came up here after school and never left."

"Clown college?"

She chuckled in spite of herself. "English major. Duke University."

Marco whistled. "Tell me about the puppets. I might have need to hire them again."

"College. It started as volunteer work in Durham and the university hospital. Now it comes in handy to augment my income."

"Which comes from free-lance writing."

"Yes. I was hoping you'd mention that in the article I thought you were writing when you lead me to believe you were a reporter."

"Here we go again."

"You can hardly blame me."

"I'm thinking of blaming you for a lot of things, but that's beside the point. Sarah Brant did mention it. Her article was in this morning's business section. Grand opening, local artisans, educational toys, all the usual. She highlighted your performance, something to the effect that your career is in copywriting and public relations. It ran as a caption under the photo of a little guy spellbound at a picnic table." Marco smiled. "Of course, he could have been spellbound by me."

"You'd like to think so."

"You have to admit we made a great team. There's no harm in the fact that I got an earful of insight into your goals and aspirations. There's no harm in knowing you want to make your mark in this business." He leaned over his desk. "I'm the first to admit that Amanda's a demanding boss. It's her way of getting the best out of people."

"I'd just as soon you didn't mention this to her when she gets back. Feel free, however, to leave the newspaper article on her desk."

He laughed. "I will."

"I have another appointment. I'd like my check."

"Karen has it at the desk."

"Good. I'll get out of your way."

"I'm not at all sure Mendenhall and Lipton wants you out of the way."

Lindsey's look of pleasure made him smile. His phone buzzed. "Hold that thought and hang on for a minute." A local printer with a question about typeface for a brochure was on the line. Marco held up his finger to Lindsey as he listened, but she tapped her watch and left his office.

At two o'clock a clearly agitated Lindsey walked from the Rodney Square branch of her bank back down to Stowman Place. The spring wind whistled and whipped off the water and she made a mental note to pack Alex's jacket for baseball practice. For the second time that day, Karen showed her to Marco's office.

His back was to her. He was on the stool, bent over his drawing board, engrossed in a design. Classical music was blaring from the corner boom box. When she cleared her throat and got no response, she entered his office and put her hand on his shoulder. If it startled him, he didn't show it.

It startled Lindsey, however. The familiarity of the gesture was unlike her. She wasn't used to analyzing her behavior, and certainly not her motives. Nevertheless, despite protests and denials, there was a bond of intimacy between them that seemed natural.

Marco turned his head and grinned. His disarming expression was a combination of surprise and pleasure, the same expression she'd observed countless times during their puppet performance.

"Lindsey. I've been expecting you. Looking for a signature on that check?"

"You knew? I was in line at the bank before I realized that you hadn't signed it. Marco, if that was some sort of ploy—"

"Ploy?"

"To get me back here."

"To get you back here, all I have to do is offer you an assignment."

This time she did flush, embarrassed at the inanity and implication of her remark. "After yesterday, I don't know what to expect from you. I'm sorry."

"I tried to signal you when I was on the phone. I meant for you to get the check from Karen and bring it to me. I thought you were just going to the ladies' room or something while I was on the phone. By the time I realized the mistake, you'd left, and by the time I got out to the sidewalk you were nowhere in sight. Where did you go, by the way?"

"Eleventh Street. Another client."

"Competition."

"A woman has to eat."

"Good. There's something we have in common. How about an early dinner? We could continue to resolve our differences."

"No, thank you. I have to get home. My appointment with the opera society dragged on much longer than I'd planned."

"The opera society. Do you go to their performances?"

"They give me complimentary tickets occasionally. Are you a fan?"

"It runs in the family. Opera is mother's milk to the D'Abruzzi clan."

"I'll keep that in mind." Lindsey handed him the check and tried to ignore the fact that he looked delighted.

"What do you do for the society?"

"Newsletter, brochure copy, fund-raising twice a year. Whatever needs to be farmed out. Today was last-minute changes in copy, proofreading, discussing upcoming events for the next issue. Pretty dry stuff."

" 'Don't knock the bread and butter.' That's a direct quote from the founder of M & L. It's what keeps us going, too. There's nothing like gloss and glamour on the top, provided there's a healthy base of steady work."

"I'm as good with one as with the other."

He laughed. "I'll bet you are." He handed her the check. "I can't change your mind about dinner?"

"No, really."

"Late lunch?"

She shook her head.

"Is there a husband waiting?"

Lindsey held her breath. This was by no means the first time a business associate had shown a personal interest in her. It was her own interest that bothered her, her own pulse rate and heartbeat. "No husband."

"Significant other?"

"I don't combine my social and professional lives."

"You're turning me down out of principle."

Those principles were usually easy to fall back on, a given from the first month she'd been self-employed. She watched his sinfully thick eyelashes lower over his inquisitive eyes. He looked at the floor, or her shoes, or some nebulous spot on the industrial carpet. "A woman with principles."

"Lots."

He smiled. "If I weren't in a position to offer you business assignments, would dinner be a possibility?"

"But you are, Marco."

"I suppose that means I have to keep hiring you in order to see you again."

Lindsey's heart thundered as she feigned composure. "I guess it does."

He laughed softly, as if he were amazed with himself. "Principles."

"Lots."

Marco took the check from her and signed it as the company vice president. When he handed it back, their hands touched. "To be honest, I've been pursuing this because yesterday I got a somewhat different impression of you, *from* you."

"You were mistaken."

Marco sighed. "I was mistaken. That's it? No moral outrage, no sputtering in protest?"

"I needed your help, and I went after you until I got you. I was aggressive, I admit it, but I apologize if you misinterpreted my motives. I'm grateful for your help with the puppet show and flattered at your invitation."

"But what you really want is an assignment."

"Of course."

"Am I out of line now?"

"Marco, I suspect you've been just short of being out of line most of your life."

His laugh stayed with her as she left the office.

Five

There were days—and this was one—when Lindsey couldn't decide whether her situation as a free-lancer made her life simpler or infinitely more complicated. At four-thirty, as she knelt and pulled a sweatshirt over Justin's head, she thought about working full-time in an office. Having an employer would give her the luxury of concentrating on her career for a full day, with her children in reliable child care after school.

However, even if she could find a suitable child-care program, or Mary Poppins, for that matter, it would stretch her already precarious budget to breaking. She thought about a part-time job, one that would get her home before the school bus and not require sitters' fees. She had the equivalent of that already and it exhausted her. She was in her own catch-22.

It was a mental discussion she conducted with herself regularly. Today, however, there was one more element she kept considering, and reconsidering. Marco D'Abruzzi made her feel as transparent as cellophane, with a little color perhaps, some texture, but translucent. Those thick-lashed eyes looked through hers, into crevices and recesses she felt a sudden need to protect.

The sexual tension—she couldn't think of any other term that came close to describing it—had ignited the moment he'd crossed the room at the bookstore. There was no point in denying it. She knew he'd felt it. Unfortunately, she knew that he knew that she'd felt it as well. She was courting disaster. Oh, to be back in clown white and billowing costumes.

She finished the day catching the end of Alexandra's baseball practice, while the twins scampered on the nearby playground equipment. She forced aside thoughts of Marco. Her afternoons belonged to her children, time she set aside free of assignments, meetings and fantasies of creative directors. These moments were precious.

Baseball was her oldest daughter's passion, and her determination to play on the Little League team tugged at Lindsey's heart. Half a dozen girls had agreed to sign up, but only one other had followed through, and she had been assigned to another team. After the first week of practice, Lexie had insisted that she was to be called Alex. By the second week, Alex insisted that she was only to be dropped off and picked up. No family member was to come and watch.

Lindsey had yet to determine whether the problem was lack of skill, lack of confidence or bullying by some pint-size boy who thought girls belonged in the softball league. One more worry.

At five-thirty she drove the little family home and turned into the driveway as Justin unsnapped his seat belt and vaulted into the front seat. "I want Chicken For Supper."

"You're in luck, Jus—we're having chicken for supper."

"I mean Chicken For Supper, Mom, the 'don't fight, eat right, ten pieces in a bucket, that's a super picker-upper.'"

"You watch too much television."

"Andy Stern's mom buys it every night on her way home from work."

"Goodness, every day he gets sodas and snack cakes, and every night take-out fried chicken. He must be the luckiest guy in first grade."

"I told you."

Alex shook her head as they got out of the car. "Can't you tell when Mom's kidding, Justin? She thinks all that stuff'll rot your teeth and goop up your heart."

"Only thing that goops up your heart is Ryan Hammel."

"Ryan Hammel is none of your business, nosy."

"'I sat next to him on the bench for half an inning. It was heaven.'" Justin's singsong quote brought a scream of outrage from Alex. "'He thinks Lexie's a baby name, he likes Alex better, so I'm Alex from now on.'"

"You listened to my phone calls, you little sneak! Mom, he's been snooping when I talk with my friends!"

Justin yanked open the car door and flew into the backyard, with Alex in hot pursuit. Brooke ignored all of it and crossed the street to a group of neighborhood children.

"Come in when I call you," Lindsey called to anyone who might be listening, and wearily headed for her kitchen and the chicken casserole nobody wanted to eat.

Once they were at the table, she reprimanded Justin, and discussed rights to privacy with all of them. However, she decided to leave the issue of just how much Ryan Hammel meant to Alex for a quiet time. Lexie to Alex because a boy liked it better... She watched her daughter eat for a moment and shook her head. It was too soon for male trouble, too soon for both of them.

Dinner, showers, Alex's homework and refusal to discuss Ryan, her insistence that everything was fine, the twins' science project and bedtime stories accounted for the evening. It was nearly ten by the time Lindsey brewed herself a cup of herbal tea and headed for her tiny office, a former sun porch that flanked the living room.

Her business-phone answering machine was blinking. She pushed the Play button, startled at the pleasure produced by the sound of the voice pronouncing her name. "Lindsey? It's Marco. Give me a call when you can. If it's after six, try me at home, 555-5512. I never sleep."

D'Abruzzi, 555. The number he'd left was a rural exchange which included Dorset Mills. She thumbed through the Wilmington directory, curious to discover where a creative force like Marco D'Abruzzi might live. Drst Ct. There was a twinge in her chest. She read the listing twice and pursed her lips at the painful coincidence. The address had suited Jonathan perfectly. She couldn't picture a Hawaiian-shirted advertising executive having anything to do with it.

Lindsey dialed Marco's number. On the fourth ring she expected a tape machine to kick in, but instead got a groggy, "Hello?"

"Marco?"

"Lindsey?" There was a perceptible yawn.

"Did I wake you? Your message said you never sleep."

"A ploy to make sure you'd call. Long day. I guess I was dozing over some paperwork I brought home." His voice cleared. "I'm glad you called." This was followed by a protracted silence while he shuffled papers. "Since the only way I can see you again is over an assignment, I'm offering you one."

The man pulled no punches. "I'm not sure that's the way Amanda runs the agency," she replied.

"You've wanted to impress her, here's your chance."

"Marco?"

"You need to eat, you're desperate for accounts, remember?"

"What are you offering?"

"Unfortunately, only work."

"Very funny."

"We landed the Tri-County Energy Commission account this afternoon. Amanda's been after it for a year—wining and dining them over lunch, the whole production."

"Go on."

"She finally made a formal presentation about two weeks ago. She was a hit. I called her in Seattle and gave her the news. Now I'm out to impress them and her by getting the first of their projects on the boards as soon as possible. We need a copywriter, of course. You fit the bill."

"Shouldn't you run this offer past Amanda?"

"To tell you the truth, it was her idea."

"Really?"

"On my mother's lasagna. Could we talk about it tomorrow, over lunch?"

"I don't do lunch."

"In this business everybody does lunch. Business lunch, Lindsey."

"I have another deadline. Lunch cuts up my day, takes too much time. I need it to write. The best I can do is breakfast."

"I'm doing the hiring. Hasn't anyone told you when an offer's involved, the agency vice president calls the shots?"

"I can't say as anyone's ever mentioned that."

"Nobody does breakfast."

"I do." She smiled at the grumpy tone in his voice.

"At what unholy hour?"

"Jump-start your day. How's eight-thirty?"

"In the morning?"

"I'm worth it. Stop all the unprofessional grumbling." She sighed at the ease with which the repartee flowed between them. "Marco, one more thing. If I consider it, we have to have an agreement."

"*More* stipulations?"

She fought the temptation to mention flirting and innuendo. It would only lead to flirting and innuendo, even over the phone. She sighed again instead. "No stipulations. Tell me about the assignment."

"In the morning."

"Fair enough. You make the coffee, I'll bring the muffins."

His laugh settled at the nape of her neck. "Heck no. We're going to do this right. Office coffee and deli muffins are for follow-up appointments and turning in copy. I'll see you in the Brandywine Room of the Hotel DuPont."

"For heaven's sake, I only meant something light in your office. A restaurant isn't necessary."

"I'm calling the shots, remember?"

Six

Marco fought another yawn as he watched Lindsey sip her coffee. The dining room buzzed with subdued conversation from the business people and hotel guests as she glanced at the N. C. Wyeth painting on the nearest wall. He would have preferred dinner with her in the hotel's English pub. He would have enjoyed conversation more intimate than discussions of deadlines and typeface. Nevertheless, he'd gotten further than he'd expected.

Even though he'd been ten minutes early, he'd found the woman waiting for him in the hotel lobby, looking like a misplaced sunbeam. No serious pinstripe suit, no business heels, no briefcase. Her lemon yellow oxford shirt was open at the throat and tucked into buttery gabardine slacks. She had leather flats on her feet and small silver hoops in her ears. The light hit the crown of her head and diffused into a dozen shades of gold. Her smile made him grin, all too sleepily.

"No one should look so perfectly perky this early in the morning," he said as their orders arrived.

"First impressions are everything. Even if you were to suddenly adopt a banker's wardrobe, it's that Hawaiian shirt I'd remember."

"If it's first impressions you're after, you've left yours, too, right down to your purple fingernails and chartreuse sneakers."

"I'm sorry I brought it up."

"Not to mention the lavender nose."

"It made an impression. That's all I was after."

He wanted to tell her how deep that impression went, how thoughts of her had lingered Sunday as he'd gone off to his tennis match, how her presence had teased him in his empty office after she'd picked up her check, how long the sound of her softened syllables played in his head after they'd finished their phone conversation. He was not, however, a fool when it came to pleasure or business, and Lindsey Major was a volatile combination of both.

"I suppose wherever we go from here, there's no forgetting our first business encounter," he replied instead, rubbing his hand through his hair, then smoothing his rumpled sports jacket.

"You're looking subdued this morning. No Hawaiian prints? No banana trees?"

He brushed his silk tie, which on close inspection proved to be a pattern of multicolored fish from knot to point. "A power breakfast with a client in the

Brandywine Room calls for something more conservative."

"Barely." Her laugh was husky and full, as powerful as a first cup of coffee.

They sampled English muffins with various marmalades, and a fruit plate. Lindsey grinned as she put down her coffee. "Delicious, but time's awastin'. Tell me everything."

"Colombian beans, no doubt brewed and steeped by DuPont kitchen elves. Homemade muffins, too."

"That's not what I meant."

He tapped his chest. "City boy, Boston's North End. You know about the family's proclivity for opera. Also rabid Red Sox fans. Academic scholarship to Boston Academy. Football scholarship to Lehigh University."

"Not that, either." Her effort to look disgruntled fell short as she pulled a pad and pen from her purse. "Everything about the business at hand. Open that portfolio you propped at your knees."

"The assignment."

"Let's get down to business, Marco."

"If you insist."

"I do."

He pulled up his zippered case and opened it. "The coordinator is a guy named Mark Desmond, their PR director. They're about to embark on a five-year program of conservation education, special projects aimed at specific targets. He wants to start with a packet on recycling for students in the Delaware schools, public and private. For the lower grades I'm designing a comic-book format." He pulled the storyboards from his portfolio. "This design was part of Amanda's presentation. They've approved the concept." He tapped the series of black lines that indicated copy. "Now I need specifics to go with my design. For the older grades, we use the same characters in a different format."

"More copy."

"Yes. You write everything for both reading levels, to accompany my art."

She pushed aside the breakfast dishes and looked it over. "Sounds promising. Once I make my current deadline, I could take it on. Can you spare the boards for the next few days? I'll start on it tomorrow night, Wednesday. How about if I come back with something Friday morning?"

Marco leaned back. "Can you turn something around that fast?"

"A rough, yes."

"I'm impressed."

"A person has to eat."

"So you've mentioned. I like desperate writers, the lean and hungry ones. Gives their work a certain edge."

"Who else were you considering for this assignment?"

"Nobody, unless you can't handle it."

"I can."

"Any conflicts I should know about?"

Lindsey paused, but said, "No."

"How about puppet shows planned for the near future?"

"They don't conflict."

"I asked only out of curiosity."

"The children's librarian at the Bancroft Parkway branch of the library wants to set something up for her story hour on Sunday afternoon."

He grinned. "Let me know if you need a partner."

Lindsey suddenly glanced at Marco. "You were a good one." Just as quickly, she lowered her head and studied his mock-ups.

Marco blamed his heart rate on the caffeine. If ever there were a woman who could get a man started in the morning, he was sitting across from her. In the course of this single conversation her voice had gone from cat's purr to forthright and back, with the speed of insight. She hesitated when he thought she'd be decisive and she was adamant when he thought she'd acquiesce. His entire body was on edge, invigorated from scalp to toe.

She continued to look at his work, and he handed her the second set of illustrations.

She looked them over with deliberate care. "Clean, crisp. I like your style."

"Subtle but deliberate."

"It lends itself to different reading levels."

"My style?"

She smiled. "Your designs."

He nodded. No small talk. His quip about the library hadn't elicited much more than a raised eyebrow. She took a final sip of her coffee as he leaned over and pulled notes from his case. As he straightened up, he caught her watching him. Over the cup, her glance was a duplicate of the aquamarine stare from under the false eyelashes he'd seen that fateful

Sunday afternoon. Lindsey Major had a glance that was open, sensuous, a path to incredible possibilities. Less than forty-eight hours earlier that glance had first mesmerized him. Once again it vanished with a blink, hardly more than a figment of his fantasies.

"I'm going to enjoy this assignment," she said finally.

"No more than I am."

Lindsey groaned and pushed at her hair. All she had to do was finish the thirty-second radio spot for the opera society and she could begin the M & L assignment. Nothing clever came to mind, however—no turn of phrase, no play on words. She swiveled in her chair and stared at her computer screen, then at the gallery of family pictures on the bookcase.

She always made a point not to discuss her children with business associates, and Marco wasn't to be an exception. Single or childless professionals like Amanda Mendenhall and Marco D'Abruzzi didn't need ear infections and strep throats as excuses for missed deadlines, facts of life though they might be. Mentioning her kids in the same breath as a business conflict struck her as unprofessional, certainly not something any male free-lancer would do.

At the moment, all three children were bursting with health and at school for hours more. She hadn't been thinking of them, even as she stared blankly at their pictures, despite the fact that she couldn't concentrate. What came to mind kept her grumbling and fighting hot flashes.

Lindsey Major, the professional, was an astute judge of character, especially of the creative, hard-driving types she dealt with daily. Well before the fateful puppet show, instinct and a good look at the creative design work at Mendenhall and Lipton had made her anxious to pursue the account.

It had never occurred to her that Lindsey Russell, the woman, would have to fight her own imagination before she could even settle down at her computer. She had to dismiss the image of Marco D'Abruzzi that kept swimming up from her subconscious. She had to dismiss the memory of his voice and his wit. She had to forget that she'd danced her puppets over his spine, into his hair and around his chest.

Something was brewing in her, something she continued to blame on the man himself, because it was inconceivable that it could emanate from her. It wasn't the first time she'd been inexplicably drawn to a man the moment she'd spotted him. That's what worried her the most.

The sight of Jonathan Russell across the Duke University campus had mixed adrenaline and pulse into a giddy combination she thought would last forever. She'd misjudged herself as badly as she'd misjudged the object of her affection. Her woman's intuition and raging hormones were a deadly combination, one that had led to disaster and heartbreak.

The turmoil of life with Jonathan, the separation, the guilt, the reconciliations, the grief over his death, had smothered what was left of her emotions. So she had assumed.

Work was all she wanted—the chance to write for Amanda Mendenhall, not the agency's five-foot-eleven-inch combination of bravado, talent and irreverent curiosity. Marco D'Abruzzi could charm a rosebud into bloom. A wave of desire began a slow, steady spiral through her chest until her breasts tingled beneath her cotton blouse. Even alone in her office, Lindsey flushed furiously and stood up. She walked to the window and studied the thorny tangle climbing over her neighbor's fence.

At five-thirty that afternoon, one glance at Alex's slumped shoulders and hesitant walk was all Lindsey needed to assess her daughter's mood as the youngster left her scattering teammates and climbed into the car.

"Hi, darling," Lindsey began. "I wish you'd let me come and watch your games. I'd love to see you play."

"There's nothing to see, don't you know that? Don't you know I'm the strike-out queen?" The child blinked angrily and swiped at her tears with the soiled shirttail of her uniform.

Lindsey leaned to hug her, but Alex shouldered her away and pulled on her seat belt. "I don't need any dumb hugs! I'm not a baby. I just want to go home, okay?"

The rebuff threatened Lindsey's composure as well, but she put the car in gear and started driving through the parking lot. "We'll get you into a hot, soaking bath. That'll help."

"You always think you know what'll help! Nothing will help. I stink at baseball. It's not for girls. I never should have signed up."

"I bet it's Ryan Hammel who calls you the strike-out queen," Justin piped up from the back seat. "I bet he's the one who said you stink."

"Shut up!"

"You shut up... Lexie."

"My name's Alex, you jerk."

"Mom!"

"That's enough from both of you."

"Mom, say something. You always punish me for saying shut up. Aren't you going to punish her?"

"Enough!" Lindsey pulled to the side of the road and counted to ten. "Alex, apologize to your brother. I know you're upset."

"No, I'm not!"

"Justin, try to understand. Even grown-ups say things they don't mean when they're angry or hurt."

"Yeah, like you and Dad, and look what happened," the boy replied.

Lindsey closed her eyes and pressed her forehead on the steering wheel. Her throat burned and her eyes stung.

"Now look, you made Mom cry."

Lindsey swallowed. "It's all right. It's just that I'm tired, and not in the mood to arbitrate between siblings, that's all."

Justin still leaned over the seat. "What's *arbitrate?*"

"You can look it up when we get home, after you put your seat belt back on and sit down. You two make me sound like a broken record." She patted her daughter's knee. "It's all right, Alex. Justin, I know how you feel about your dad's death. It was a car accident, darling, which had nothing to do with the fact that he didn't live with us, or that we argued."

"Or said things he didn't mean or you didn't mean. You've told me a million times," he replied from the back seat.

"And one of these times, I hope you'll start to believe it."

"He was good at baseball. He could have helped Alex."

"Yes, he could have, and that's one of the ways we miss him. Now let's get home before Brooke gets dropped off from Brownies," Lindsey replied as she put the car back into gear.

Seven

"Marco, it's Lindsey Major."

"Hello." Lindsey! Surprise, pleasure and anticipation drifted through him like warm molasses. He settled into the couch, ready for the retorts and one-upmanship he was beginning to associate with their fledgling relationship.

"Is it too late to talk business?"

"Never. No problems, I hope." He paused at the catch in her voice. "Lindsey?"

"Bad day. Fatigue is all. I'm sorry to bother you at home."

"Not on my account, I hope."

"No."

"Are you overworked, trying to finish that deadline to get started on ours? If so, Mendenhall and Lipton can wait. Make yourself a hot toddy and put your feet up. Call me in the morning. Better still, give me your address and I'll make you one."

"I'm fine, really." She sighed, and he pressed the receiver closer to his ear, inching himself backward into the down cushions, kicking off his moccasins.

"Friday was your idea. Take the weekend, if you need it."

"No, it isn't that. Marco?" There was a catch again, and a deeper sigh.

"Talk to me."

"No. I shouldn't have called in this frame of mind. I have—" she cleared her throat "—another call. I'll be right back."

Before he could reply, the line was put on hold. Concern mingled with the pleasure as he waited again, perplexed.

"Marco?" Lindsey's voice broke his reverie as she came back on the line.

"I'm right here."

That seemed to make her sigh again. She blew her nose. "Thanks for waiting," sounded as if it came from beneath a tissue.

"Talk to me," he repeated, curious as hell. The woman so determined to convey the image of steely independence was obviously fighting for composure. It unglued him. Women's tears always did, and the image of Lindsey alone at a desk, forlorn and depressed, was so unexpected, it made him ache.

He forced back the impulse to take over the conversation. Unconsciously he stroked the throw pillow, as if it would offer comfort. He'd spent the better part of the afternoon analyzing Lindsey Major's quicksilver personality and her obvious need for privacy. He knew better than to expect her to confide in him.

"Thanks. Really. It's nearly ten. I shouldn't have called, I just had a question or two."

"You shouldn't be working this late. What's got you so beat, or defeated?"

"Nothing, really. It was a mistake to call."

"The hell it was. You're not yourself. Tell me why." He glanced at his watch. "Give me your address and I'll be right over."

He'd imagined her office a dozen times since breakfast. Sometimes he saw it clean, crisp, modern; sometimes casual, crowded, cluttered. Always Lindsey was in yellow, shades of butter and lemon, as she'd been at the hotel.

"No, no, I'm fine, really. I called to ask about your storyboards. I'm having some trouble interpreting the second and third frames of the first board, and the last panel of the second. I should have had you go over them with me before I took them." Although it was obvious that she was making a concerted effort, her voice settled from tremulous back to the steadiness he was used to.

"Are you just looking them over now? It's late to be starting something fresh, especially if the assignment has you all strung out."

"Marco, don't worry about my hours."

"I'm worried about the assignment," he lied. "If you're really going to work late, I'll be happy to come over and interpret. Strictly a professional call, on M & L's honor."

There was a long pause. "I shouldn't have called. I can tell I've worried you. You think I'll blow this assignment and you'll have to answer to Amanda. I won't let you down, Marco."

"See that you don't."

"Yes, sir." She managed a soft laugh.

"You should do that more often, you know. Yours is one of the five-star laughs. It's one of the best."

"Marco—"

"And I know laughter."

"You've got this all wrong. Honestly, it had nothing to do with the assignment."

He brought the pillow to his chest and broached a subject he knew she'd never raise. "Is it finances that have you so upset? You've mentioned that ever-present need to eat. M & L would be happy to advance you your fee."

Maybe there was no office. Maybe she worked from a crummy little studio apartment somewhere. Her phone-book listing was simply Wilmington, Delaware. Her business card—he'd found three in Amanda's files—listed a suburban post-office box at the Talleyville branch, the same area as her phone exchange, north of the city limits.

"No, thank you, really, I just had a question about your designs."

"How long have you been in business for yourself?"

"Marco, Amanda's already interviewed me."

"I was just curious."

"You always are." A touch of cheerfulness crept into her voice. "Three years full-time."

"Before that?"

"Before that part-time. That's enough third degree, Sherlock." She hesitated. "Could we get to the point of my call?"

"That's what I've been trying to do."

"Stop playing detective. You're right, it's late and I am tired. Could we get to the boards, please? Put a lid on that curiosity of yours."

Marco's heart had been pounding as he pressed her. Well before this he'd tried to write it off as curiosity. He was curious as hell about her, but curiosity didn't explain the physical rush at the sound of her voice, or the sudden pump of desire at the sight of her.

Her voice was clearing, but the layer of melancholy was still undeniable. One glance at those expressive features of hers, one look into those hooded eyes would give him answers no amount of compassionate questions on a telephone would elicit. He swallowed his frustration.

"Lindsey, I'm probably as beat as you are and I really need to see the boards to understand your questions. Before you turn me down, listen to my suggestion. If I can't come over, then consider this. While Amanda's out of the office, why don't you use it? Bring my designs in and work at her desk. I'm right in the office next door if you have questions. It's more efficient, plus you'll get done faster and paid sooner."

"All right."

He bolted into a sitting position. "All right? Just like that? I don't have to browbeat you, drown you with compassionate arguments about why it would be in your best interest, come over and bodily drag you down there?"

"No. I think it makes sense."

"I'll be damned. I think that's the first time you've agreed with me."

"On that one thing." She laughed, and this time it was throaty, deep and tantalizingly familiar.

"You sound better."

"I feel better."

"Good. Now tell me why you really called."

"I knew you'd explain the boards."

"I haven't yet, and you've admitted you're better, anyway."

"So I have." Again, there was no hesitation.

Marco sank back into the cushions and grinned. The woman was full of surprises. "As simple as that?"

"It's been a long, exhausting day. By the time I got to your assignment and realized I had questions, I was too tired to try to figure them out. I shouldn't confess it, but it was easier to call."

"You were on the verge of tears a minute ago."

"Never."

"I know the sound of a woman coming unstrung."

"Marco—"

"I'm a connoisseur of women. I pride myself on understanding feminine quirks and female temperaments."

"Connoisseur! I'm not a bundle of quirky temperaments—or whatever you said."

"You should know I grew up with three sisters. I've shared studio space with women, even an apartment once. They don't make business partners any more female than Amanda. I've had more than my share of exposure."

"And—let me guess—more than your share of romances have honed your skills to perfection. Women are as moths to a flame, where you're concerned."

"How flattering. Is that the image I project?"

She laughed sardonically. "Never mind what you project. This conversation wasn't meant to be personal."

"Fascinating creatures, all of you."

"Fascinating or not, if the offers still stands, this creature needs to be at a desk about eight-thirty tomorrow morning. Can you open the office that early?"

"Either Karen or I will have the welcome mat out."

Eight

"Moths to a flame," Lindsey murmured as she entered the agency the following morning, storyboards and briefcase under her arm. There was a quickness in her step and a lightness in her chest she didn't want to attribute to the previous night's conversation, but there was no other explanation.

Contentment was an emotion she rarely thought about. Her years of happiness had been mixed with resentment and frustration left too long to simmer inside her. She'd lost the art of spontaneity. Marco D'Abruzzi, however, had not. He made her feel good. He'd made her feel better. He made her feel feminine, unaccountably female.

Those female juices shot through her as Marco welcomed her. He was dressed in a fresh blue shirt, a new shade favored by her fashion-conscious children.

His tie, a silk, designer-dyed number of questionable lineage, was around his neck, but untied. His pressed slacks were gray, the only conservative thing about him—and that included his smile. He welcomed her with it and a gesture toward Amanda's office.

"Bonjour," she quipped in self-deprecating French as she preceded him.

"French. Fluent?"

"Hardly. *Très chic,"* she added as she looked at him.

"Grazie tante. Lei è molto gentile. Me or the office?"

"You, actually. That's quite a tie."

Marco rolled it up and put it in his pocket. "I avoid them generally, but I've got business later, with another client. It does make a statement. *Ah, la cravatta."*

"Perfect Italian?"

"Yes, I am a perfect Italian."

She was beginning to think he was. "Also humble. I like that in a man."

"Ah, but Lindsey, you and I know there's no place for humility in advertising. Boldness, confidence, creativity, yes. I apply it to my wardrobe, too. Clothes make the man. And what about you, a veritable ray of sunshine?"

Lindsey sighed and glanced at her own outfit. "Clichés, so early in the morning?"

"I figure a healthy dose of flattery will get you off on the right foot."

"My right foot's on the assignment. Could we get to it? I'm on a tight schedule."

"Scusa."

"In English."

"Just trying to melt a little ice here."

Lindsey grinned in spite of herself. "Signor D'Abruzzi, there's no doubt in my mind that you could melt an iceberg, given half a chance. Now if you'll *scusa*—" she slid past him "—we can get down to business. Could we review these, please?"

"I'm looking forward to it."

She laid the storyboards on the desk and put her copy next to it. The suddenly serious tone of his voice made her glance back at him. "So am I. I think we'll make a pretty good team on this."

"Then let's get started."

She grinned again—broadly. She couldn't help it.

By midmorning the following day Marco's suspicions were confirmed. They made a terrific team. They were compatible. *Simpatico,* he would have told her, had he had more encouragement. Had he had any encouragement he would have kissed her by now, into erotic oblivion. There were boundaries to be observed, however, neatly drawn ones dictated by business propriety, common sense and the gratifying realization that his instincts were sound. Lindsey Major was an excellent copywriter.

In the course of the previous morning she'd displayed the sixth sense every professional team player needed to complement another's work. She seemed to feel what he felt and to anticipate his concepts. Their progress had been so strong and steady, he'd gone on to propose a brainstorming session for the next phase of the project.

Standing next to Lindsey, leaning with her over his artwork laid out on Amanda's desk, made him feel like a kid again, scuffing his sock feet across a wool rug. Sparks snapped between them, sharp and quick as static electricity.

By their second morning together, her laugh came easily, and what he read in her glance encouraged him, even if she didn't. After half an hour of consultation, he left her to her work and returned to his drawing board. Their offices shared a common wall and he wasted long moments conjuring up visions of Lindsey on the other side.

At eleven-thirty she knocked on his open door and handed him her copy. "Could you take a look at this? I'll be leaving soon."

"Short day."

"Long day, actually. I've got other things to work on."

He read over the copy with Lindsey at his shoulder. She smelled of some light cologne he couldn't name, faint and enticing and completely her own. He knew better than to comment on it, however, and forced himself to concentrate on the task at hand.

"This is good," he murmured. "Great," he added, pointing his pencil to a line here and there. He looked up occasionally, and when he smiled at her, she smiled back.

They stood shoulder-to-shoulder over the storyboards and discussed two versions of a caption. Captions! He could barely keep his mind on them. When they reached the last frames, Marco sat down on his stool and checked his watch.

"How about lunch before you take off? We'll miss the crowds. There's a great Italian place where I can continue to impress you with my fluency."

"Sure."

He straightened up. "Just like that? No heavy persuasion and hours of convincing?"

"I'm hungry," she replied with a grin.

"You do keep a man guessing."

"Marco D'Abruzzi," she replied with a laugh, "I suspect keeping one step ahead of you would be a full-time job."

"Such flattery."

Marco described the antipasti as they walked and suggested some of his favorites. They were seated immediately at a tiny, linen-covered table at the window. He acknowledged the nod of a favorite waiter, who greeted him in Italian as he seated them.

"*Buon giorno,* Marco."

"*Buon giorno,* Dominic."

"*Vuole mangiare alla carta?*"

"Ah, English, Dom. Lindsey and I'll have the usual."

The waiter smiled at Lindsey. "He makes me practice the English. I let him practice his Italian."

"Is it as good as he tells me?"

"Perfect."

"How Italian are you?" she asked Marco as they were served.

"The D'Abruzzis have been here since the 1890s, but my mother's family came during the war, from Trieste, on the north shore of the Adriatic near Venice. She's kept us fluent." He paused and grinned. "Who's kept your French fluent?"

"Very funny. I struggled with three years in high school."

"You don't do any of that creative writing in French?"

"It's tough enough in English."

"Your writing's excellent."

Marco kept the conversation centered on business for the rest of the meal, getting back to the specifics of their shared assignment. He wanted her comfortable, as comfortable as he was. Lindsey's enthusiasm for her work was the natural key to the flow of dialogue that bounced back and forth over the antipasto and minestrone.

"We should be able to wrap things up Monday morning," she said as she finished her espresso.

"The printer's ready. I want to get the roughs to them by Tuesday morning and start on the booklet for the upper grades. Can you give me more time next week?"

"Some."

"Elusive, as always."

"I suppose it's my nature."

He caught her eye again over her raised mug. "Not in your work. It's clean, straightforward and to the point."

"Thank you. I take a lot of pride in what I do."

As she continued talking, he leaned back in his chair and savored the moment. He wanted more of these shared glances and sly grins. He wanted more humor, more of every aspect of her. Lindsey Major made him feel good in ways he'd been missing for too long. Nevertheless, he held back. Desire tugged, as it had from the moment they'd played together. *Too soon*, he told himself for the hundredth time. *Too soon*. Unconsciously he sighed and forced himself back to the matter at hand. He loved listening to her soft pronunciations and faint accent. Her words went through him, into his bones, into the sinew and muscle of his pounding heart.

He'd found something in this woman, something that filled a space that suddenly felt hollow, a space he hadn't realized was there, empty and waiting.

Lindsey made him feel centered, self-centered, he realized—focused on possibilities and desires he hadn't known before.

"Marco?"

"Sorry. You were saying?"

"I was saying that your design style is unique. Do you ever paint for fun?"

"I think about book illustration sometimes. Children's books, although I don't know a thing about kids."

"Draw on your own childhood."

"It was a good one. Lots of family."

"Did they support your career choice?"

"Heck no. College was fine, but they wanted me to be an engineer or an accountant. My old man's strictly union. He wanted to make sure I could feed myself."

"You do that very well, I'm sure."

"Right, now that I'm settled with Amanda. The partnership's a nice sense of security, as long as the accounts keep coming."

"And the free-lancers don't foul them up."

"You're as good as any I've seen. Faster than most, too."

She smiled. "Do you ever exhibit your artwork, outside the office?"

"Some."

"What medium?"

"Acrylic, oils. I've sold a few things in the Clothesline Fair in the past. I've had a couple of one-man shows in some galleries in town and out in Chadds Ford."

"Anything coming up?"

"Nothing planned. There is a gallery in Centerville that seems anxious to show my stuff. I haven't had the time to pull anything together."

"Please let me know if you do."

He arched a brow. "A date?"

"I'd come and toast the man of the moment."

Nine

Hours later, back over his drawing board, Marco smiled. "I'd come and toast the man of the moment." Lindsey's flirtatious reply had been the perfect opening for an invitation. Instead, he'd gone on to reminisce about his childhood love of knights and castles, and a possible story line for a book illustration. She listened to every word, added her own fantasy of a not-quite-fierce dragon looking for a castle full of lords and ladies to scare, whose scales kept falling off. They'd talked like collaborators, developing plots and themes, and all the while he'd ached like a lover.

It had taken every ounce of self-control he possessed not to suggest dinner that night, a movie or a picnic. Instead he'd let her remark drift between them expectantly, pleased that she seemed disappointed at his lack of response, sure that she would have turned him down out of principle. He had a better plan for Lindsey, one that incorporated the element of surprise.

At two o'clock Sunday afternoon, Marco tiptoed into the children's room of the Bancroft Parkway Library and worked his way down the K-3 Fiction aisle. He stood unseen among the parents and watched the clown at the far end of the room. She moved silently in all her purple-and-pink glory, knee-deep in spellbound preschoolers. The room was still, with the exception of smothered giggles, as the children imitated her.

The children finally burst into clapping and cheers, while Marco waited and sighed. For once he didn't fight the erotic memories of Lindsey's touch as they stirred his body. Gooseflesh tingled along his spine; heat spread across his ribs. It was no longer arousal from an enticing stranger, however. Now the reverie had a face, a laugh and a personality as etched in his mind as her touch. Her elusiveness was fuel to the fire.

As the children scattered, Marco moved up behind her, gave fleeting thought to impropriety and said, "Looks as though you're without a partner again today," as he walked his fingers up the middle of her back.

There was a blur of lavender as she spun around. "I beg your pardon?" she gasped without a trace of a Southern accent.

"Lindsey?"

"Betsy O'Hare."

Marco grimaced. "Her partner."

The clown frowned. "Do you know Lindsey?"

"Yes ... certainly!"

The woman relaxed. "That was quite an introduction. You look shocked enough for both of us. You just missed her. We finished our act about twenty minutes ago. This is just my pantomime workshop with the children."

"I'm sorry. I don't usually... Whatever you were thinking..." He stopped and swore silently. "I'd appreciate it if you wouldn't mention this to her."

"May I ask who you are?"

He hedged. "Your stand-in."

One purple eyebrow arched in reply.

At nine o'clock Monday morning Marco sat engrossed in his work, bent over his drawing board as he shaded a rough sketch with a gray permanent marker. He sang along with a familiar song on the radio, finally able to concentrate on something besides his impulsive nature and its possible repercussions. "Women," he muttered, fully aware that it was only one who played such havoc with his life.

As he laid the last layer of shading over the illustration board, a sixth sense made his scalp tingle. Before he could turn around or finish the lyrics, the touch of fingers coursing up his spine contracted his body into sweet spasms of shock and arousal.

He swore as he lost his balance, dragging the marker across his meticulous sketch. By the time he turned around, Lindsey was staring, horrified, at his ruined work.

"Marco, I'm sorry! Look what I've done." She was flushed from throat to cheeks, already reaching across him to the table. "I only meant to give you a taste of your own medicine, for scaring Betsy half to death yesterday. I'm sorry, really. I never meant—"

He kissed her. As if it were the most natural thing in the world, he pulled her into his arms and covered her mouth with his. The pressure of her breasts against his chest made them both gasp for breath and deepened the pleasure she'd incited in him. His mouth grazed hers with a heat that threatened her balance. As if he sensed it, he tightened his arms around her.

"You sure know how to get a man's day started."

"Marco..." Her breath caught as she panted softly. "I never meant for this to happen. You've got to believe me. We can't—"

"We just did. My God, Lindsey, I've ached to kiss you since that first afternoon, since the first time I felt your touch."

"You hardly know me."

"I know what I feel, and I've got a damned good idea about what you feel, too."

"What we feel doesn't have anything to do with it."

He kissed her again, hard, soaking up the urgency as she kissed him back. He let her go, however, when she pulled back. "Lindsey, you've wrapped yourself in enough intrigue to keep me at the edge of frustration, but I know your strengths, your talent. I know your personality, your spirit, and since the very beginning, I've sensed your fear." As she blinked and tried to look away, he cupped her chin. "I know you're fighting this as hard as I am."

"We can't do this."

"Kiss? Enjoy each other's company? Lindsey Major, if either one of us had fewer professional ethics, we'd be making love right this minute, up against those file cabinets or underneath my drawing board."

From the moment Lindsey left his office and sequestered herself in Amanda's, she knew their convoluted relationship had jumped to a second plateau. Marco confirmed it with a glance as he walked to the coffee machine. There was no clown suit to hide behind, no Pan-Cake makeup to mask the glowing blush or billowy costume to hide the pounding heart. Her reaction to this man had been frighteningly instantaneous. The kiss had been proof and he knew it. She beat a hasty retreat at noon.

Tuesday morning she arrived to find that he had business out of the office. Wednesday was the same. He had meetings with clients or printers the entire time she worked there. Lindsey wasn't about to ask Karen how deliberate the timing might or might not be.

Thursday she arrived anticipating the same. The day was warming up and her shining hair was windblown. She was wearing a faded pair of jeans with a crisp cotton shirt, open at the throat. The sleeves of a pink sweater were tied over her shoulders.

Marco was at his drawing board. There was such pleasure in her surprise that she stopped short. His glance was hooded, tentative, but he waved suddenly, heading toward his office doorway. It made her smile.

"Good morning," he said as he crossed the foyer. "A little milk, one sugar for your coffee?"

"Tea, preferably with lemon," she replied as she entered Amanda's office.

He followed her. "That's a change."

Lindsey put her briefcase on the desk. "We can't have you thinking I'm too predictable."

"Predictable is not a word I'd use to describe you. I could come up with a few others, if pressed."

"Such as?"

"Talented, creative, independent—"

"Thanks. You're an excellent judge of character."

"Elusive, coy. Confused."

"Wait a minute."

"Overwhelmed . . ."

"Enough. I'll just go get that cup of tea."

He touched her arm. When she stopped, he gently pulled the knot of her sweater sleeves into his hand. "Just as I am."

"Marco—"

"I've stayed out of the office. Haven't laid eyes on you in days. Do you know how it felt just now to see you again?"

"No." The lie made her heart race. She knew exactly how it felt.

"Raging adrenaline's a great feeling." He patted her sleeves back into place, obviously encouraged by the color seeping across her jaw from her open shirt. "Except for the fact that I hardly sleep anymore, and you ruined my Monday night tennis match."

"I did no such thing."

"My mind was elsewhere, to put it mildly. Stupid mistakes, double faults, missed points, one right after the other."

Lindsey stepped back. "I hope your tennis partner suggested a long, cold shower."

"Tried that, too. I chilled this overheated body into submission under icy spray, but it didn't work for long. I'd like to think your days haven't been much calmer."

"Marco, you mustn't talk like this, or think like this, either, for that matter," she whispered as she tugged him out of Karen's line of vision. "I'm just fine, thank you."

"Your adrenaline behaves?" He laughed in a low, throaty voice, which threatened her composure all over again.

"My adrenaline is none of your business. I've been working, afternoons and evenings, too, sometimes."

"At not thinking about how we might combine this business and pleasure?"

"The two don't mix and you know it. Now let me get my tea and let's get started."

"We've gotten started. Work now, and let's go to lunch again. Dominic's been asking about you."

She stared at him wide-eyed and smiled once more. "What is it?"

"You're very sexy, you know. It ruins my concentration. I wish you weren't so damned appealing."

"Am I?"

"Yes, Marco, you are, and we're not going to do a single thing about it."

Ten

Saturday night, unfashionably late, Marco yawned as he entered the foyer of Dorset Mill. The historic building had been refurbished along with the apartments, and was used for social and charitable events. His name tag, in perfect calligraphy, was the only one still lying on the table next to a magnificent arrangement of spring flowers. Amanda and her agency largesse, Marco thought as he picked up his tag.

M & L had provided all the floral arrangements for the advertising council's annual dinner dance, and Amanda had strong-armed him into promising he would represent the agency. The evening was networking under the guise of a social event, one he would have preferred to leave to his business partner.

Music and the low roar of conversation that earmarked such gatherings tumbled from the open doors of the function room. The noise reminded him of anxious Canada geese in a bare Delaware cornfield.

"Marco D'Abruzzi, Mendenhall and Lipton," he muttered as he read his tag and stuck it on the breast pocket of his uncharacteristically conservative blazer. He should have asked Lindsey to come with him, made it clear it was business related. Another yawn pressed at his jaws as he imagined having to get through an entire evening with her and still pretend there were no sparks. Agony.

As it was, he'd worked all afternoon over his drawing board, determined to regain the concentration fantasies of Lindsey Major drained from him.

Before he entered the function room, Marco crossed the wide, worn boards to the river side of the building and a deserted hallway next to the rest rooms. Even over the din of the guests, the whine and whip of the Brandywine hitting the mill wheel outside the thick brick walls was unmistakable. The clear, star-sprinkled night was unseasonably warm, painfully romantic. He stood at the window and watched the spring-swollen river race past, flashing under the undulating lights from the rooms around him. The artist in him automatically framed a section of the wheel caught in shadow, and another of a beech tree leaning toward the water. He lingered, not because it was picturesque, but because he was in no hurry to mingle with the throngs of co-workers he competed with daily.

"Anything worth painting out there?" The soft, honeyed drawl was unmistakable, as recognizable behind him as it would have been in front of him. Marco turned to find Lindsey, head cocked, half smiling, three feet behind him.

"I'll be damned," he whispered.

"I was on my way back from the ladies' room. I thought you looked familiar. Although in a blazer and tie, one can't be sure." She brushed his sleeve. "Have you been hiding out here all night?"

"Just arrived." He tried not to stare.

She'd swept one side of her hair back with a black velvet clip. The rest of her was draped in something deceptively simple, which caught the light as she moved. She appeared to be all green satin and silky legs. Her mandarin collar was open to the base of her throat and long sleeves began as gathered puffs on either shoulder. Her waist was cinched with a wide belt. Chin to knee, she was the color of emeralds.

"You make quite a study yourself," he added.

"Overdressed? I never know about these things."

"Perfectly dressed."

"Thanks."

"You never mentioned that you'd be here."

"No, I didn't."

He waited, but she didn't add anything more.

"Your dress is the perfect color for that dragon," he said.

"Dragon? In our story?"

He nodded and, rude as it was, let his eyes rove over her. "You are something to behold tonight."

Lindsey pressed her fingers against his lips. "Stop that. Marco, really. You make me self-conscious."

"*Conscious* is what I'm aiming for—conscious of what's going on between us."

"The place is crawling with our associates. This isn't any more appropriate here than at the office."

"I know it as well as you do. That's the reason I didn't ask you here in the first place. You're a hell of a pleasant surprise, however. What are you doing here?"

"The same thing you are. I'm a member of the council, of course, but I hadn't planned to come, hadn't even remembered it was tonight until the opera society public-relations director coerced me into it."

"I didn't realize you were coercible."

"Only under certain circumstances." She glanced around the empty space and said to the window, "One of which is not at the finale of one of my puppet shows." She stood next to him, glancing out into the night. "Betsy's been grilling me all week."

"And?"

She turned to look at him. "There's nothing to tell her." They dropped into silence as they watched the light play on the turning water wheel. Marco sensed her growing tenseness when his shoulder brushed hers.

Lindsey suddenly cleared her throat. "Dinner was about to be served as I left."

"Will you join me? You can trust my behavior in a room full of people." Marco crooked his arm, and when Lindsey slipped her fingers through it, he patted them. "Although I was hoping I wouldn't be able to trust yours."

The music started as dessert was served. Dinner conversation had been pleasant, if stilted, as he'd tried to stay clear of controversy. Lindsey had picked at her food and now took a mouthful of sherbet as he slid his chair closer. "I never waste a waltz."

"Your sherbet will melt."

"You might enjoy yourself. It's only a dance, Lindsey."

It wasn't just a dance and they both knew it. It was an invitation to break down the already tenuous barrier that she continued to keep between them. Marco was on his feet next to her chair with his hand out.

"If I step on your toes, we'll sit down," he promised.

She swallowed and put her spoon in the saucer. "I might step all over yours."

"A risk I'm willing to take."

They danced. As they circled the crowded floor, they chatted for a moment, then slipped into silence—again, that silence. Lindsey was an excellent dancer, fluid, smooth and confident. "No puppets this time," he said as she slid her arm along his shoulder.

"Not this time."

Marco tightened his arm across her back and steered her away from another couple. She moved closer into his arms and stayed there, near enough so that her breasts brushed his chest and her hips occasionally grazed his. He tried to think of something light to carry the conversation away from how warm and wonderful she felt, but couldn't.

Lindsey stopped attempting conversation. Instead they danced—really danced—to one, then another, romantic tune from the big-band era.

"You're good," was murmured in his ear.

"Wednesdays, in the gym at St. Margaret's. Some mother in the neighborhood decided we needed exposure to the finer things in life." He laughed. "Thank you, Mrs. Del Vecchio, wherever you are. How about you?"

"The Raleigh Sociables, Thursday afternoons."

When the band finished the set, he looked at her. "That wasn't so bad, was it?"

She looked at her feet and back up at him before responding. "No crushed toes." Without explanation, she excused herself to go to the ladies' room.

Marco left the room, as well, and went back to the window where he'd first run into her. As he propped his elbows on the railing and watched the floodlit river, she came out of the rest room and stopped next to him. He turned and looked at her. The intensity of her glance worked its magic on him. He listened to his pounding pulse, felt the sweet stirring of his body. The urge to touch her swept through him.

He leaned forward and kissed her, forcing himself to keep it excruciatingly light. For good measure he jammed his hands into his pockets.

She sighed and turned to the water. "I knew that would happen."

"I wish you'd told me. It would have saved a lot of wear and tear on my anticipation index. I'm sorry I didn't kiss you way back when we were standing here earlier, for that matter."

"We shouldn't have done it, even now."

"There's a river out there perfect for walking beside, and a fat moon hanging in the trees."

"I've seen the moon."

"You've been quiet."

"Yes. Too many people, I guess."

"I live right next door. If I promise nothing but conversation, would you come up for coffee?"

She blanched, remembering suddenly his listing in the phone book. "You live at Dorset Court?"

"Don't look so shocked. I don't suppose I fit the mold. Amanda found it for me. Her family has all the connections to this place. She's old school, old money...."

"I'd rather not."

"Then walk with me. Conversation's all I'm after. French, Italian or English. Your choice."

She smiled. "No, really. I'd like to go home."

"It was only a kiss."

"It has nothing to do with you, Marco, or very little."

"And all this time I thought I was the cause of tonight's romantic introspection."

She smiled. "I'm sorry I haven't been better company."

"Let me be the judge of that."

"I think I'd better go. I have my car."

"I'll walk you that far."

"I'm fine. Go finish your dessert."

"Only to your car, Lindsey."

"All right. I suppose you know how persuasive you can be."

"One of my biggest strengths."

"The sherbet will be mush."

"The rest of me's not much better."

Eleven

They followed the stairs down to the riverbank exit, into a rush of fresh air sweeping off the water. Lindsey shivered.

"I have a remedy for that."

"I'm sure you do."

Marco put his arm around her.

"Is that it?"

"How much warming up do you need?" he whispered.

"Your arm around my shoulder does nicely."

"Too bad."

No pressure. No pretense. She was dangerously close to contentment despite the location and its associations. They walked in silence along the footpath, which separated the landscaped bank from the courtyards and entrances to the restored mill-workers' houses. She got as far as a familiar set of granite benches when déjà vu clutched her. She fought a shudder.

"Aha, maybe a single arm around your shoulder isn't enough, after all. Could I suggest something that generates more heat?"

His gentle humor brought her close to tears. "I should go. You wouldn't understand."

"You'd be amazed at how much I understand, once someone speaks to me."

"Marco, I'm sorry. This is lovely, really—romantic. You know that."

"Always a but." Before she could continue to protest, he leaned over, his voice low and close to her ear. "Lindsey, this should have been a quiet dinner someplace, after hours. You should have been dancing in my arms without a room full of business associates tracking us."

"But we are business associates, Marco."

"Not on Saturday night."

"There's a Monday morning after every Saturday night."

"Heck of a motto."

"Marco, Saturday night with you, any Saturday night, would complicate any hope of the—how did you put it?—clean, straightforward, to-the-point work you complimented me on last week. Things were bad enough after the kiss in your office. You know as well as I do that you can't mix business with pleasure. What happens when one element falls flat and drags the other down with it?"

"You're too pragmatic."

"I'm a realist, and a professional."

"Who's been trembling in my arms."

She pulled farther back.

"Pulling away won't work, either. I've tried it myself."

"What we feel—this intensity—is just sparks. You know that."

"It's your sparks I feel, Lindsey."

"Raging hormones settle down sooner or later."

"I don't want them to settle down. I don't want to get over this. If it's happening too fast, then we'll slow it down. We'll start with lunch or dinner, a walk, a movie—something simple. A picnic, tomorrow. Or maybe another kiss," he added with a grin.

She put her fingers over his lips again. "We are what we are. Don't jeopardize the relationship we already have. We're business associates first. I need that, Marco, more than... the other."

He groaned softly at her temple. "'The other' might be a very pleasant diversion after a long day of business."

"You and I have different priorities." She broke from him and continued toward her car, fighting the lump that burned at the back of her throat.

Marco came beside her again and put his hand gently on her shoulder. "It isn't just me, is it? Have I behaved like a jerk tonight, insisting that I know how you feel, just because I know what I want?"

"Your behavior's fine. Flattering, as a matter of fact."

"All this time I've thought you were quiet because you were fighting the mad, passionate desire to give in to your baser instincts and seduce me."

She laughed softly. "You do have a way about you."

"What's eating at you? What's all the stuff you insist I wouldn't understand?"

"I don't want to discuss my private life. You'll just have to accept that I don't want the two parts of my life to overlap. We work beautifully together. We get along fine. Can we be friends, real friends?"

"Passion aside, we are already, or we wouldn't have the relationship we already have, the one that took about fifteen minutes to feel absolutely perfect. You wouldn't have called me in tears the first week I knew you."

"It was a long day. I was tired."

"No matter how you analyze it, or ignore it, even then you wanted the sound of my voice, and I was damn glad of it. That's the honesty I want between us."

"If you can't have anything more, would you settle for that?"

"What I'll settle for isn't relevant to what's eating at you tonight. It's more than fighting feelings for me."

She scanned the landscape, washed in moonlight. "This place holds memories, that's all. I thought I was over them, otherwise I never would have come here tonight."

"Friends confide in each other. If it was a rotten love affair, tell me about it. You're entitled to a few."

"Marco..."

"You don't give a guy much to go on, but I've assumed you're divorced, not that I can imagine anyone in his right mind giving you up."

"You don't understand."

"I hope you threw the bum out on the sidewalk if he didn't treat you right."

"Marco." He stopped and she raised her face to the stars, blinking hard. "I'm a widow." She stood still, listening to the peepers and the soft *whoosh* of the narrow river. Marco caught his breath and she knew he was searching for words.

"It's complicated," she continued when he stayed silent. "We were separated at the time, with the divorce pending. I was trying for a reconciliation."

"Lindsey—"

"It's all right."

"How long has it been?"

"Nearly two years since we separated. He died last spring." She walked the remaining distance to her car and stood next to the passenger door as Marco reached her.

He put his hand along her cheek. "I'm so sorry."

When she nodded, he cupped her face and kissed her. The feel of his mouth against hers made a shambles of every good intention. Relief hadn't come with the cold water she'd run over her wrists back in the bathroom, or the air she'd dragged into her lungs, or the resolve that she'd never repeat her mistakes. There hadn't been any relief since the moment she'd played puppeteer, not since she'd watched Marco

D'Abruzzi's bemused expressions and felt the warmth of his cooperative body.

"You can start to put it behind you," he whispered. "Don't leave yet. You need to talk and I need to listen, more than we need anything else. Stay with me for a while. Please trust me, Lindsey."

His voice was salve to a wound. The night was early and her sitter didn't expect her until midnight.

She was struck with the image of her daughter working her baseball glove, Alex pressing her small fist, or the ball itself, into the supple leather. "The fit has to be just right," she was always telling Lindsey. In Marco's arms, the fit was just right.

Desire dissolved the grief. She stood, pressed against her car with the waterwheel and the river in front of her, and Marco caught in the pools of light. He shone, from his hair and eyes to the heat in his touch.

"Even if there were nothing else to keep us apart, I don't know if I'd be any good at this."

"You're very, very good at just being Lindsey. That's all I want."

He put his hands to her eyelids and closed them. She parted her lips and he traced her tongue. He kissed her face and her mouth, then deepened the kiss—or she did. She didn't know, didn't care. Kissing Marco was a lesson in her own sensuality. He seemed to be moving in slow motion with her, waiting, building desire by layers. She touched his hair and he wove his fingers through hers.

"Come sta?" He kissed her lightly. "How are you?"

Even in English there were no words for the turmoil. "How do I answer?"

"Benissimo, grazie. Che sorpresa!"

She looked into his shadowed face. "Which means?"

"Very well, thank you. What a surprise."

"You speak for both of us."

The kisses started again, at her jaw, her ear. She arched her back and tightened her hands on his shoulders in surprise.

"I know," Marco said softly. "I know."

Marco fixed them short drinks, and settled into the down cushions of his couch with her. His head spun with questions he dared not ask, afraid she'd bolt into the night if he pressed her. She offered no more than glimpses of her past as he listened, holding back his curiosity and his frustration. He kept the lights low and the music off as she talked. Again she faltered.

"I'm having a tough time with this," she murmured.

"I know."

"I mean *this*." She gestured at the room. "You should probably know that it was home for Jonathan and me."

He choked on his brandy. "The Dorset?"

"In all its glory. We had a one-bedroom apartment that faced the mill. Bride and groom. I thought it would last forever. After we separated, Jonathan sublet one of the studio units at the other end."

"And you?"

"I kept the house. By then we'd moved down to York Road, off the Concord Pike."

"How did he—"

"Car accident."

"I've imagined all sorts of things about you, but I never would have come up with this. Have I been too damn flip all this time? Too damn self-centered?"

"You've been wonderful."

There were no tears, but she changed the subject and asked about his background, pressing and prodding for information. His stories of art school and parental disapproval held her interest, so he showed her his makeshift studio, set up in the second bedroom.

"This is my second office and where I do the fun stuff." He talked about city life in Boston and his partnership with Amanda, his family, sisters and brothers-in-law, nieces and nephews. She began to relax, to examine bits and pieces of the eclectic room. She picked up a paintbrush, then a tissue-paper overlay from an illustration. Through it all she studied him in that way that heated his blood all over again.

"Have there been many women in your life?"

"A few."

"Never been married?"

"More than one would tell you that making a career out of design and advertising has taken most of my time and too much of my energy. I've had this vague idea that I'd do something about it when I reached thirty. It's creeping up in another year. Now I'm thinking thirty-five."

"You seem the family type. House full of kids all drawing and painting at the kitchen table."

"Me? Children aren't high on my priority list. I have a tough enough time taking care of my own needs. You put me in a panic the day you talked me into playing the clown. I had no idea how they'd react."

"They loved you."

"They loved *you.*" He let the words linger between them and watched her lower her lashes. For the first time since they'd entered the apartment, he touched her. He wove his fingers through hers and held them against his chest as she looked at him.

"This room is so full of...you, Marco."

"It's where I do my best creative work."

"Is it?"

His jaw tingled, then his shoulder. Heat pressed his ribs. "There is one more room, across the hall. There's a bed, all the protection we need and a man who wants you more than you can imagine."

Without a word, Lindsey brought his hands to her breasts.

"Are you sure?" he whispered.

"I'm not sure of anything anymore."

Twelve

"Close your eyes," he whispered, "and try to imagine how wonderful you feel to me." He began to run his fingertips in circles over the sheer emerald fabric of her bodice. He circled her full softness with the heel of his hand. He spread his fingers, prodding the sensitive tips to nubs with his thumbs. As her body responded, fragments of desire leapt through him. This was how he had known it would be, and yet beyond anything he'd imagined.

He paused. *Remember this,* he thought. *File this away for some cold, bitter night fifty years from now. Remember how she looks and how she feels.* Even in the low light from his drafting-table lamp, he caught the flush rising from her throat and felt the sudden heat across his own jaw.

Her breathing deepened as she shuddered. Marco leaned against her, thigh-to-thigh. She arched in his arms, and the sheer emerald fabric of her dress slid against him. He held her, aroused and arousing as she moved.

"When was the last time, Lindsey?"

"There was only Jonathan."

His heart jumped as responsibility washed over him. She opened her eyes. Desire had flecked the slate of her irises with azure. "I hadn't felt anything for anybody until you."

"That," he said as he kissed her, "is the most stimulating thing you could have said. I only want what you want."

"There's no doubt that I'm going to regret this on Monday morning, but I want the here and now, and I want it with you."

He led her across the apartment alcove to the second bedroom. The hall lamp was enough to see by and they undressed each other in the sharp rectangle of light it threw into the dark room. It caught the curve of her hip and his thigh.

She stayed quiet, with her arm across her breasts as she stood with him. He heard her breath catch. Slowly she lowered her arm and cupped her hands together, moving them into the light. "When I was a child I used to think you could hold moonbeams—catch them, if you could just be allowed to stay up late enough, if you could just go outside and chase them across the lawn."

Remember this, Marco thought again. *Hold this against all the ordinary, mundane moments that have made up your life.* Her breasts swayed as she cupped the light. He looked at her palms, her tapered fingers, and ached to call up the moon for her. Her hands trembled.

"Lindsey, are you sure?"

She moved them forward. They still trembled, but she came to him. Her smile was tentative, her eyes wide in the shadows. Suddenly she began to finger-walk. "I'm sure," she replied. She moved up his spine, around his ribs, tracing the familiar trail.

"Even then, even with the puppets," he whispered. "Your hands and your eyes—"

She cupped him. The shock of her touch, the unexpected intimacy, drove a bolt of desire into him. Heat sank to his hips as he stopped talking and thrust against her. He leaned, too, and kissed her breasts as he slid his hands over her. She was warm, already swaying softly, instinctively searching for rhythm to match his.

They moved simultaneously from the light into the shadows and onto the bed. Marco stopped only long enough to pull the promised packet from his bedside table. Time fell away as they lay together, exploring, expanding the need for each other before he settled her under him. The rhythm between them was perfect, the union complete.

"Lindsey!"

"Che sorpresa," she whispered.

He laughed and kissed her wildly, abandoning himself to the physical joy. Lindsey rose to meet him, again and again while the sensations built on themselves. He tried to tease in Italian, but he couldn't think. She seemed to stroke every nerve ending in his body as she moved.

Suddenly she clung and arched and called him. He felt the pleasure slice through her, felt her savor it. She pulled him down one last time and then, suddenly, it was his. He'd reached what he'd ached for since the moment he'd met her. Ecstasy rolled through him in waves that stretched and licked like flames. Pleasure ignited his body and engulfed his heart as he made love to Lindsey Major.

For a long time afterward he lay still and listened to their breathing. Lindsey sighed and moved into the crook of his arm. His contentment was as deep as the passion. He dozed. He awoke to the feel of a kiss on his cheek.

"I'm going."

He opened his eyes. Lindsey was standing next to the bed, still in the shadows, but fully dressed.

He put his arm out. "Of course you're not going. Come back in here with me."

"You promised no pressure. Go back to sleep. I'll see you Monday at the office."

He rose up on his elbow, fully alert. "Monday? What happened to tomorrow, a picnic at least, a drive someplace, out to Chadds Ford? We could take in one of the art museums."

"I need some time, Marco. I need tomorrow to make sense of this. I don't expect you to understand, but this happened so fast. Nothing's clear. If you really care about me, you'll give me time to work this out."

"You're giving me no choice, so go ahead, work it out," he said reluctantly. "I won't pretend that you at my door at the end of it all wouldn't make my night."

Lindsey did go on a picnic Sunday afternoon. Marco, however, was not invited. At three o'clock, after watching Alex's baseball game, she brought her children back to the neighborhood park, carved from the last undeveloped lot on the corner of York and Tower Roads, and bought and maintained by the families who made up the civic association. On the far side of the playground the children played with others from nearby streets.

As they played, she leaned back against the trunk of the beech tree that sheltered her blanket and the remains of a packed lunch. A lifetime ago she and Jonathan had been part of the equipment committee, and had shopped for the swings and seesaws that filled a sanded area in the corner. Lindsey closed her eyes, but it wasn't Jonathan who appeared behind her lids. Marco D'Abruzzi's handsome face and naked body assaulted her reverie.

"Marco D'Abruzzi." She rolled the melodic combination of syllables around on her tongue as she whispered his name. *"Che sorpresa."* She'd made love to him as if it had been the most natural thing in the world. She sat against the tree and forced herself to think about what she'd done.

With her eyes closed, desire began its slow dance all over again. Marco was a link to emotions she'd nearly forgotten she possessed: the thrill of anticipation, the delight in a compliment, pleasure that spun from confidence. The man made her feel good. His lack of pretense was dangerously appealing. He inspired trust. He had from the beginning. Why else would she have called him the very first week, as if he'd been a trusted friend or confidant? Why else had she abandoned herself to everything he was offering? Why else was she leaning against a tree with her eyes closed, reliving all of it?

"What's so funny, Mom?"

The sound of Brooke's voice startled Lindsey into opening her eyes. "Funny?"

"You're over here all by yourself and smiling like Alex told one of her dumb jokes."

"Am I?" She flushed.

"You okay? You look weird."

"Certainly. Have some cookies."

Brooke stuck one in her mouth and scooped a few more into her hand as she scurried back to her friends. It wasn't dumb jokes that had Lindsey smiling, not by a long shot.

The man inspired confidence, even as he looked for encouragement. No doubt he was used to women who danced in his arms all night—young, uninhibited women who were used to expanding the moment from innuendo to something wonderfully erotic.

For a moment Lindsey sat under the tree and imagined herself one of those women, but then the smile left her. Marco might be just the man for a little self-indulgent pleasure if she were twenty-one or -two, not thirty; if she were a social acquaintance, not a professional one.

He'd be the perfect sexy, sensual diversion if she'd never been married, never been burned by the heartache of trying to maintain a failing relationship. Marco was just unpretentious and appealing enough for her to imagine the possibilities, but that was where the line was drawn. She'd been torn by regret and touched by grief as a result of the same careless emotions. To fit this fantasy, Lindsey had to be someone else entirely. There was no place for dewy-eyed romping at the possible expense of her financial security, no place in the scenario for three children in need of rock-solid stability.

"Enough," she muttered as she called the twins and got to her feet to shake out the blanket. She could have used a good shake herself.

"Boys are so weird."

"All boys or a few in particular?" Lindsey smiled at Alex's reflection in her dressing-table mirror as she wound her daughter's hair into a French braid. At five o'clock the youngster was fresh from the bathtub and smelled wonderfully of herbal shampoo.

"Well, all brothers are weird, so that includes Justin, of course, but mostly I meant Ryan."

"Ryan Hammel, star slugger?"

"Yeah. That was some home run, wasn't it?"

"Yes. And that was some triple you hit right before him."

"That's what I mean. Ryan's always telling me I stink at baseball, but this afternoon, when Adam Peterson said something mean, I heard Ryan tell him I could hit one out of the park if I felt like it."

"And what did he say when you nearly did?"

"Nothing. That's what I mean. He sort of smiled, but that was all. Adam Peterson said I was awesome, though."

Lindsey hugged her. "You are awesome, Alex, just the way you are. You mustn't let the opinions of boys affect what you think of yourself."

Alex looked at her braid and stood up. "You're not going to tell me all that stuff about how there's lots of things I'm good at and some things I'm not so good at, and I shouldn't worry about other people, are you?"

Lindsey laughed. "I guess you already know all about it."

"I know I hit a real good triple run this afternoon. I was glad you saw it. I guess I want you to come to my games, after all."

"It was awesome."

"Did Dad ever tease you about not being good at things?"

Lindsey paused. "Skiing. Your father always wished I were a better skier. I guess he teased me some, yes."

"I hope you're not going to get a lot of boyfriends now. Sarah Dougherty's mom has a ton of boyfriends and Sarah has to spend the night at her cousin Jessica's all the time cause her mom has sleep-overs. Jessica's a total pain. She's six and she goes through Sarah's stuff. They have to share a room. Sarah says it's gross."

"You're not Sarah, darling, and I'm not her mother. I don't have sleep-overs."

They were interrupted by thumping as Justin raced up the stairs and appeared at the bedroom door. "Jill's here. There's one piece of cake left and Brooke says it's hers."

Lindsey shook her finger. "Tell Brooke it's big enough to be cut in three, and it's not to be touched until after dinner. I'll be right there."

Thirteen

Lindsey stood outside Marco's apartment entrance for long, introspective moments before she rang the bell. She was in the same jeans she'd had on all day, with nothing fresher than a starched shirt. He wasn't to think she'd done anything more than stop by.

Behind her the river raced and memories rose to haunt her, some distant and painful, others fresh and erotic. The combination threatened to overwhelm her.

Her children were with their favorite sitter, Jill Crenshaw, a University of Delaware day student who also lived on York Road. Still, Lindsey had agonized over the fibs and excuses of going to see her business associate on a Sunday evening. She shifted from foot to foot as she searched for a reason that would justify her actions.

Marco opened his door looking remarkably shocked and painfully handsome. "You are full of surprises."

His dark eyes shone as he grinned. His hair was still damp at the edges from an obvious shower. He had on khakis and a loose shirt, with gray socks. Her heart thundered at the sight of him and she was reminded all over again of the endless possibilities he represented.

"Hi," she said for lack of anything clever. "Am I interrupting?"

"My normal heart rate? Yes. Come on in." Marco put out his arm.

She shook her head. "This isn't what it looks like. I've come to talk. I probably should have called, but you promised no pressure." As if enough of her senses weren't already assaulted, the minute she crossed the threshold she was accosted by an aromatic cloud wafting from the kitchen. The apartment smelled deliciously of something sweetly sour.

"Pineapple?"

"Good guess. I've got a sauce simmering in there that could use a feminine touch."

"Smells to me as though it's doing fine."

"Are you?"

She shook her head. "I've done nothing but think since I left you."

"Not always a healthy idea."

"You make it hard. You make it hard to do anything but *feel*. What happened between us Saturday night...there's no denying the chemistry, Marco, but it's not—I don't know—appropriate. It jeopardizes my professional situation with you." She looked away as he clenched his jaw. "You make me feel unstable. I don't know who I am when I'm with you."

There was more. She'd rehearsed all the way over, reason after reason, each of which evaporated as she looked at him. How could she explain anything to him, when she could barely make sense of it herself? As badly as she wanted him to understand her responsibilities to her children, her real life, she wanted—needed—him ignorant of all of it, felt he *had* to be separate from all of it.

Marco's eyes were dark. "Before you continue about our professional situation, take a look in my studio."

He did nothing more than put his arms on her shoulders to nudge her in that direction. Nevertheless, his warmth was electric.

The room was as she remembered it, with the exception of the drawing board. Pinned to the four corners was a rectangle of high-quality paper. It was covered with an intricate pen-and-ink design, half of which was painted. The sketch showed a bird's-eye view of a walled medieval town, except that it wasn't a bird, it was her flying dragon. Marco's conception had brilliant emerald scales and lemon-to-buttershaded wings. The creature had a familiar grin and gleam in its eye.

Below the dragon's magnificent wingspan was everything she'd described so briefly. Flags waved on tents, knights in full regalia jousted. Marco had filled the paper with lords, ladies, artisans, peasants, dogs and horses, all of whom seemed to be eating, selling wares or celebrating. His colors challenged the rainbow as much as his design challenged imagination.

"It's not finished, of course, but what do you think?"

A lump had formed in her throat. "I can hardly believe it. This is remarkable."

"It's your story."

"It's your design."

He pointed to the queen, who bore a remarkable resemblance to herself.

"Me?" Lindsey looked closely at the gown and headpiece, painted in half-a-dozen shades of yellow and gold.

He tapped the paper. "Those are the colors of the outfit you wore that first day. The dragon's the color of your dress at the mill. Silk in my hand."

"Marco, you mustn't."

"It's done. We've begun, Lindsey."

She stopped again as she spotted two jesters entertaining a crowd. They were dressed, crown to toe, in the purples and patterns of her clown outfit. "Us?"

"In half-a-dozen places. What do you think's going on inside that tent behind the jousting arena?"

Tears welled from the corners of her eyes as a thousand sensations seized her. Erotic currents snaked through her, released finally from the grip she'd maintained at home, on the drive over. Her flush was instantaneous.

Marco held her, making it impossible to deny the shudder and the ache. He kissed her temple. "It's worse than ever, isn't it? Worse because Saturday night was perfect."

Anticipation intensified the pleasure and embarrassed her as Marco put her at arm's length. A look of pure contentment eased over his face as he smiled. "Oh, Lindsey," he whispered. "Oh, darling, I know."

Marco slid the sheet away and rolled to his side as Lindsey's breathing slowed. She was quiet now, but minutes ago the urgency had been electric. From hallway to bedroom, they'd played, petted and kissed until the pool of desire had become a caldron.

He'd felt his own heart pound against the swell of her breast. Her pulse matched his. She returned every caress until rhythm racked their bodies. Once again Lindsey had moved with him, against him, as they built the passion, layer by layer, then raced toward its climax. It came simultaneously.

It was long moments later that Lindsey slid her hand along the curve of his hip and drew lazy circles with her thumb. Her skin was damp between her breasts where he'd begun the lovemaking. He pushed the hair from her face and kissed her. "You make a person forget, Lindsey, everything but the essentials."

A red chamois shirt lay on the back of the chair and she pulled it on. He watched the lamplight play across her bare thighs as she walked back to his studio. When he looked at her, contentment lay so deep that he caught his breath. When she made love to him, it was dangerously easy to forget how much she'd been through, how tough the road had been, how little she offered beyond the passion. Her body responded to his in a way that belied her attempts at privacy. What he ached for now were her words, the recognition that she was offering the same thing as he. Love.

He pulled on jeans and crossed the hall to her as she looked at the drawing table. "My story, your illustrations," she whispered as if she were trying to make sense of it.

Marco glanced at her in his soft, worn shirt. She seemed oblivious to the fact that she filled it out in ways no man ever could. It fell to her hip and was open to her breastbone. He put his hands on either side of her face. "There are many things we do beautifully together. We've discovered only a few of them."

Lindsey looked at him wide-eyed. He got lost in her gaze, deep as a moonless night, fathomless, full of a need she would never mention. He kissed her and slid his hands inside the flannel. Dinner was delayed, but delicious.

He didn't broach the subject until they were side by side at the sink, rinsing the last of the dishes. "Stay," he said simply.

"I can't."

Marco put down the plate he'd been holding. "We work like partners born to the task. We make love as if there's no end to passion. Yet you won't—"

"Don't push this."

"If I had a decent reason from you, I wouldn't."

"That's why I came here tonight, to tell you that you're overwhelming. *That's* overwhelming."

"As if going home alone to your own cold bed gives you some sort of ridiculous safety net? Don't you know what I see when I look at you? Don't you know what's in your eyes, what's in your body when I touch you?"

"That's enough."

"You can't get enough. Neither can I. There's a reason and you know it as well as I do."

"I shouldn't have come over here. I should have called and talked on the phone like a reasonable person."

"Come on, Lindsey. You don't honestly mean you regret this."

"I don't know what I mean. You make me feel like someone I don't know. Can you understand that I need some distance from the intensity?"

"No, I can't."

The tension spilled over into Monday. As Lindsey arrived at Mendenhall and Lipton the next morning, Marco was hunkered over his drawing board, trying to look thoroughly engrossed in work.

"Marco?"

The sound of his name in her soft Southern accent increased the frustration. Nevertheless, he raised his coffee mug in salute. "Good morning."

"Good morning."

He glanced at Karen out at the desk. "Look, I'm sorry. I know you think you know what you're doing."

She put her hands on his drawing board. "This is just the kind of thing I was afraid of. We can't—"

He leaned forward and kissed her with the board, an open jar of rubber cement and a sheet of type between them. The kiss was interrupted by the thud and scramble of pencils rolling off the table onto the floor as Lindsey's elbow hit the container. She knelt to scoop them up. He knelt beside her.

"We can. We have already. This is wonderful. You're wonderful. We're not the first two people to mix business and pleasure." He touched her arm, encouraged by the heavy-lidded glance she gave in response. "If I push, it's because I'm impatient." He stopped as she put her fingers against his lips.

"Marco, this isn't appropriate office conversation."

"Let me be the judge of what's appropriate," he replied through her fingers. "We can arrive in separate cars in the morning, if you're concerned about propriety."

"I don't do lunch and I don't do sleep-overs."

He laughed in spite of the tension and straightened up, bringing her with him. "You've made an exception to the first. It's time for an exception to the second."

"No, really."

"Not allowed out on school nights?"

"This is happening too fast."

"I appreciate everything you've been through. I understand. You mesmerize me, you and your intrigue."

"It isn't intrigue."

"Most women—"

"I'm not most women. You know as well as I do we've been running on pure adrenaline and hormones since the day we met. You've taken everything I have to offer."

He winced.

"I have work to get back to."

"Women," Marco muttered for the fiftieth time as he hunkered over his worktable. He was as tight as an overstrung violin, with a headache coffee had made worse.

Before she left, Lindsey had had the decency to tell him she was going back to her home office to work.

"In full retreat," he'd replied, not regretting it until well into the afternoon. She'd already proved to be the writer he was looking for, the writer Amanda needed. Passion and frustration had to be secondary to that important fact. He knew that. If free-lancing from her home office would keep their decidedly unprofessional relationship separate from their professional work, so be it.

The day was overcast and misty, but by late afternoon, the sun broke through and all signs of puddles were gone. The entire area was in full bloom and Marco left the office determined to take advantage of it. *Spontaneity.* The woman who personified it was about to get an apology along with a taste of her own medicine.

Fourteen

———

York Road was in a picturesque community of compact houses closer to Wilmington than Dorset Mills, but on the same side of town. He knew the street and he knew Lindsey's car. The rest he could figure out himself.

He left Karen to lock up and picked up a deli picnic before heading north along the Concord Pike, just ahead of the evening traffic. The moment he pulled off the busy thoroughfare onto the suburban streets, skaters and tricyclers replaced the heavy traffic. York Road curved and crossed with others in a sea of blooming dogwood and cherry trees.

"Suburbia in full flower," he said, dissolving his preconceived notions that Lindsey might live in an avant garde exception. There were no exceptions. Each house was a narrow, charming colonial adaptation of the one next to it, the uniformity broken only by the meticulous landscaping.

He slowed his bright red sports car to a crawl and continued along the curve of York Road, searching for her familiar compact sedan. He spotted it in the driveway of a white brick interpretation of the housing style and parked behind it. A mountain bike lay in front of it.

The door closest to him seemed to enter into the kitchen, and as he stepped up on the stoop, the incessant buzz of a timer came through the screen. The main door was open, the screen door ajar. He knocked on the frame, which barely made a sound, and cupped his mouth.

"Lindsey?" The familiar, unmistakable smell of his sweet-and-sour sauce wafted from the stove. He could see the pot. "I'll be damned."

Some warm and yeasty fragrance blended with it. Muffins, maybe. He knocked again and entered. "Lindsey? It's Marco."

The reply, such as it was, came from behind him. "Excuse me." The screen door squeaked as it was pulled back. As he turned around, a boy whose head came nearly to Marco's waist thrust a bottle of laundry detergent at him. "My mom said to return this to Mrs. Russell. She said thanks."

"Mrs. Russell?"

"Alex's mom," the child replied with a withering glance. "Who else? Something's ready in the oven. Can't you hear the timer?"

"I don't... Yes, thanks," he muttered as the child jumped off the steps and disappeared down the driveway.

Marco turned back to the stove and fumbled with the timer dial, got the buzzer to stop and opened the oven. He pulled the cookie sheet off the rack with the tail of his shirt as the dining room door swung open.

"Hey! What are you doing in our kitchen?" a tousle-haired girl in a baseball uniform demanded. There was fire in her eyes.

The cookie sheet clanked as Marco dropped it on the stovetop. "I'm looking for Lindsey Major, but I think I have the wrong house. I knocked just now and called, but the timer was buzzing. I guess nobody heard me. Your muffins are ready."

"Biscuits."

"Biscuits. Do you happen to know which house is Lindsey Major's?"

"This one."

"This one?"

"Sure."

They were interrupted by an ear-piercing scream from the second floor. "That's just Justin upstairs. He stubbed his toe, and he's acting like it's going to fall off or something. Mom's trying to get the gravel out, and he's yelling something awful. What a dork. There's hardly even any blood. He's such a baby. Mom sent me down to turn off the oven," she added as she snapped the dial.

"Lindsey Major is your mother?"

"Sort of. That's just her work name. She's really Lindsey Russell, same as us. Same as my dad was."

"Your dad. Lindsey Russell." The sound was foreign. "I'm Marco D'Abruzzi. She's doing some writing for me. Has she ever mentioned me?"

The child shrugged and shook her head. "I don't think so. She writes for a lot of people, like the opera guys and the electric guys. She's writing a comic book for the electric ones."

"That's me."

"You're Mendenhall?"

"Sort of. Would you tell her I'm here?"

Before Marco could add anything, the child disappeared back through the dining room and called up the stairs. "Hey, Mom, somebody named Mark Brucie Mendenhall—or something—is here."

Marco tried to fit the pieces together. He tried to suck in a full breath. The sweet ache of anticipation had evaporated, replaced by confusion and, now, a sick feeling of astonishment. "Lindsey Russell," he said.

The child reappeared. "Mom says to tell you that I'm Alex, and about Justin's foot. I said I already did. She says she'll call you later. She has to drive me to Myer's Field for my game."

"Does she need some help?"

"No. Thank you." This time the clipped reply came from Lindsey herself, who appeared behind her daughter. She was a disheveled version of the same Lindsey Major he'd expected to be holding in his arms by now.

"I came over to apologize. Knowing how fond you are of spontaneity, I thought I'd surprise you," he said. "I guess the surprise is mine."

Lindsey nudged her daughter's shoulder. "The tub's running so Justin can soak his foot before we go."

"He'll make us late, Mom."

"No, he won't, darling. Just run up and make sure he swishes around a little. I'll be right there."

Alex complained, but followed the order. The moment the child was up the stairs, Lindsey turned to Marco with irritation in her voice. "This is really a bad time. Very bad. I told Alex to tell you I'd call you later."

His tone matched hers in anger. "She did."

"Well, I will. Please, I've got to pack a supper, finish up with Justin, find Brooke and get out of here. None of this has anything to do with you. Please don't add to the chaos." She put her hand on his arm. "I'm sorry. I didn't mean that. I hardly know what I mean anymore. You, more than anyone, should know that."

"Who's Brooke, or shouldn't I ask?"

"I have three children, Marco. Alexandra, plus Justin and Brooke, fraternal twins."

"Three! And they're all eating my sweet-and-sour sauce."

"I know I owe you an explanation. I'll call. Really."

"Twins?" He felt like someone had rammed a fist in his gut.

"Marco, we've had a professional relationship. It began with writing assignments. That's all it was meant to be. This . . . other . . . is just—"

"You know as well as I do that it began with incredible chemistry most people never find in a lifetime."

"Keep your voice down."

"I felt it when clown paint and a crazy costume hid everything but your voice and those eyes. Those eyes, Lindsey, haven't lied since. One look from you, one touch that afternoon, and I knew you felt it every bit as deeply as I did."

"I devoted a good part of my adult life to trying to sustain those kinds of feelings in a relationship. It didn't last. I'm old enough to know these things don't."

"You're hardly an experienced woman of the world. What were you, a child bride?"

"Marco, I'm nearly thirty-one years old, almost two years older than you are."

"With no experience beyond life with and without Jonathan Major."

"Russell."

"Of course. Lindsey Russell."

"You know how I feel about you. We're having a wonderful time together, but there's no need for it to involve anyone else. All I want is what we have, moment to moment."

A piercing wail, elongated into a drawn-out "Mom!" came from the upstairs bathroom. "I've got to go. I'll call you."

"I'm not sure that what needs to be said can be discussed in a phone call."

She dropped her hand from his arm. "I tried talking face-to-face by coming to the Dorset last Sunday night. You saw how much good that did."

"I know exactly how much good that did."

"Marco, please. You can't talk like that here."

"Explain about Russell."

"I've kept my maiden name professionally to separate my private life, my family, from the rest. So far it's worked."

"Perfectly," he replied. "When, exactly, were you planning to get around to mentioning the rest of your life? Or was our entire relationship going to consist of your showing up whenever you felt the need for a few hours of heavy breathing, before disappearing back into the night?"

"It's worked well so far."

Her reply shocked him into silence.

Fifteen

"Chaos," Lindsey muttered. She fought tears as she sank down onto the hill and watched Alex fumble with the ball during her warm-up. Although Justin had insisted he was much too injured to put his bike away, he'd finally stopped limping, and had joined Brooke and other siblings of the Little Leaguers on the playground equipment.

Lindsey sat on the hill and thought about the phone call she had to make. She'd tell Marco about making his sweet-and-sour sauce. She needed a few light spots in a conversation she was dreading. A hand on her shoulder startled her back to the present.

Marco sat down next to her without a trace of humor in his expression. He hardly looked like himself.

"I said I'd call," she said, still watching the players.

"I'm not the type to sit around waiting for the phone to ring." His voice was as leaden as it had been in her kitchen.

Lindsey's heart fell. "You're upset that I didn't tell you about my children."

"For starters, you're damn right. A man's supposed to know a woman has three children when he makes love to her."

"I exercise," she whispered.

"That's not what I meant. Children, house, a neighborhood. I have no idea who you are. I'm involved with a woman who lives some kind of double life. You've been evasive since the day I met you, but this afternoon was beyond even my imagination."

"You liked it that way."

"I've let it go because I thought the reason was your husband. Poor, fragile Lindsey with her broken heart. That heart-wrenching confession about Jonathan barely skimmed the surface of who you are."

Lindsey lowered her voice again. "Your appeal is who you are, Marco. You're a twenty-nine-year-old, fun-loving, no-holds-barred bachelor, in love with life. You're certainly enamored of exactly the relationship we already have." She waved her arm at the vista. "None of this has anything to do with that."

He stared at the players without responding.

"Marco, I've needed something like this for a long time, but you can understand that I would never involve my children in anything so temporary." She put her hand on his arm. "Nobody else on the face of the earth knows me better than you do."

"That's not saying a heck of a lot. Lindsey, I don't even know who the hell you are."

Marco looked from her stricken expression out to the scattered players practicing on the field. She didn't reply and he stood up. "I guess that about covers it."

He left her on the blanket and walked down the hill. He'd stared at the playing field, then lost his focus. Nothing was in focus, least of all the relationship he'd spun from flirtation, chemistry and desire, three elements that had unraveled like a novice attempt at knitting. Novice was exactly what he was. For all his bravado and polish, he was a damned neophyte when it came to the psyche of a woman.

"This woman," he muttered.

The Lindsey he knew was little more than a figment of his imagination, as insubstantial as spun sugar. He suddenly had no idea who she was, let alone what she wanted. He walked with lead in his chest.

"Marco D'Abruzzi?"

He recognized one of the coaches as his insurance agent. The man had a clipboard in his hand, which he raised in greeting.

"Jake."

"This is the last place I'd expect you to show up."

Marco shrugged. "I played in high school. Actually, I had some business with one of our free-lance writers, who's got a kid on the team. Alex, I think her name is."

"Sure, Alex Russell. While you're here, how about tossing the ball with her? I've got my hands full and we're a coach short tonight."

"Can't, Jake. I don't think her mother—"

"Just till the game starts. She's a peppery little thing, but some of the boys give her a hard time. She's got potential, she just needs practice. Ten minutes." He handed him a glove and motioned to Alex. "Go out for some long ones. Marco'll give you some practice."

Alex Russell squinted at him as they walked to an open area. "I sure hope you can throw better than my mom."

"Not much good?"

"Not much help, that's for sure. My dad was pretty good. He always told me he'd coach my team when I got old enough for this league."

"I'm sorry he can't be here."

The eight-year-old cocked her hat. "Did you know him?"

"No. Your mother told me about him."

"Can you throw grounders?"

"I can try."

"They're my worst ones."

"Then go on out and I'll send some your way. How about fly balls?"

"I'm better at them as long as the sun's not in my eyes."

Twenty minutes into the game he was still there. Between innings and her times at bat, he worked on Alex's toss, her catch, her batting stance and, for good measure, her attitude. She was shy, but determined, with a gleam in her eye that was reminiscent of her mother's. At every glance, Marco found Lindsey on the hill, one hand on her hip, the other shading her eyes. He hadn't had this much scrutiny since the day he'd met her.

The mother of three. He threw the ball to Alex.

The mother of three. Alex threw it back.

Alex and Justin and Brooke. Marco tossed the ball.

Lindsey, Alex and Justin and Brooke. The ball sailed back and hit him in the shin.

At midnight Marco stood over his drawing board in drawstring pajama bottoms, stirring a splash of Scotch on ice with his finger. The soft tinkle of the cubes tumbling in the glass was all that disturbed the quiet. Sleep wouldn't come. Contentment eluded him.

On the board the whimsical figures grinned and winked and jousted. He sipped and put his head back to let the fiery liquid sear its way into his empty gut. He picked up a pencil and settled his stare on his red chamois shirt. It still lay on the floor where he'd dropped it. He'd undressed Lindsey, button by button. His body stirred and he tapped the metal lampshade with his pencil. She'd stood right there with light and shadow illuminating her like a Renaissance study, giving so much... and so little.

Thirty-one, three children... His body stirred, but the ache was anguish and it extinguished the desire. He finished his drink, stunned at the speed with which something that had brought him such pleasure could deliver such confusion. With a final *plunk,* he hit the shade again and shoved the pencil back into the cup.

At nine-thirty the next morning, Marco took a call in his office from Lindsey. "I just phoned to tell you that I'll be working from home for the rest of the assignment. I should be finished with it by Thursday afternoon."

"You don't need to do that."

"I do need to. Very badly."

"Distance."

"Marco, about yesterday."

"Did Alex win?"

"Yes." Lindsey paused. "I want to talk to you about Alex."

"She's got a good arm and a nice swing. Spunky kid, too. I'm sure it's tough being the only girl on the team."

"She manages."

"I understand kids give her a hard time once in a while."

"That's not your concern."

"Then why did you bring her up in the conversation?"

"I'm worried. Now she's giving you credit for a couple of good catches. She wants you to keep coaching her."

"I did give her some good hints."

"I know and I appreciate it, but . . ."

"Always the but. Throwing a baseball a couple of times a week is out of the question?"

"I don't want to involve my children in this."

He looked at Karen through the doorway, busy with paperwork. "In what?"

"You know very well what. Whatever it is we're doing."

"Are we still doing it? Care to give it a name?"

"No, I don't. The point I'm trying to make is that this whole thing will run its course and they'll be stuck. Attachments can be harder on children than on their star-struck parents."

"You don't have much experience at this sort of thing, from what you've told me."

"I have all the experience I need in parenting. You're the one who doesn't have a clue."

"Perhaps—" he twirled a pencil "—this 'whole thing,' as you call it, has already run its course."

The music from his office radio filled the dead air. "Maybe it has," Lindsey said finally.

Long after he'd hung up, Marco sat staring at the wall. He finally swore and snapped the pencil in two.

Sixteen

Lindsey hung up and gave herself the luxury of a good cry. She'd rehearsed and rehearsed her words. In the shower, at her computer, packing lunches for the kids, all her arguments had made perfect sense. She should have guessed he'd challenge every sentence that left her parched throat. She should have known better than to expect a subdued, levelheaded response from Marco D'Abruzzi. The man wasn't levelheaded about anything. Then again, if he were, she wouldn't be in the midst of a flaming affair to begin with. She blew her nose and laughed sardonically.

"A torrid affair, gone down in flames," she said out loud.

Hours later the familiar squeal of the school bus brought her to attention and forced her to concentrate on something besides her own misery. Within moments, Justin, Brooke and Alex came tumbling into the kitchen, ravenous, as always. Brooding over her recalcitrant art director would have to wait. For the rest of the afternoon, she had real life to contend with, which began by laying out snacks, looking at class papers and arbitrating arguments.

"So, is Marco gonna meet us at the field?" Alex asked between cookies.

"He can't. He's very busy."

She looked crestfallen. "Did you ask him? He said he might yesterday when he left. I told you he said—"

"Alex, you have coaches to help you."

"There aren't enough to go around."

"Then I'll work with you in the backyard, or we could ask Mr. Crenshaw."

"Right. Even you know you stink at baseball, Mom. Just because Jill's our baby-sitter doesn't mean her dad's any good. Besides, he doesn't even get home from work till it's dark."

"We'll find somebody."

"I bet you didn't even ask Marco. I bet you think he'll say no, because he gives you work that's too hard and you don't like him."

"Too hard?"

"I heard you crying in your office last night and swearing at him."

"Alex—"

"It's either that or because I'm just a dumb girl on a boys' team."

"That's not the case at all."

"Right." She left the kitchen and stomped up the stairs.

Lindsey gave herself a minute to collect her thoughts and followed Alex upstairs. She sat on the edge of her daughter's bed. "Can't you accept that sometimes I know what's best?"

"You think you know what's best, but I know what helps."

Lindsey tried to calm the unsettling combination of anxiety and desire as she watched Marco walk toward her across Myer's Field. The breeze played in his hair and teased his shirt. His shirt! The man had the audacity to wear the red chamois one she'd pulled on after they'd made love Sunday, the one he'd left in a heap on the floor of his studio.

She crossed her arms. Her breasts tingled as if he were working the buttons of her blouse. Total recall raised gooseflesh across her ribs where he'd slid his hands and worked his magic. Twice in an evening! Her cheeks burned at the memory of her insatiable behavior. The heat deepened as he reached her.

"Thank you for coming, for doing this for Alex," she managed to say.

"Mind changing is a woman's prerogative."

"We've said some hurtful things to each other."

"You've done some hurtful things. I admit I never expected to hear from you again today, not with this request."

"My daughter seems to think you made her a promise yesterday."

"And risk the wrath of her mother? I'm flattered that she thinks I can make a difference." When she shot him a worried glance he looked right into her. "I assume from that blush that you recognize the shirt. Frankly, you generated so much heat in it, I expected to find nothing but a pile of ashes where we dropped it."

Lindsey looked desperately around her. "Don't talk like that. I suppose you wore it on purpose."

"Why?"

The flush spread to her ears. "Never mind."

He looked genuinely surprised. "It's one of my most comfortable shirts, a favorite. It seems to be making you extremely uncomfortable, however. Let me give you a bit of advice. If you're going to throw yourself into passionate, no-strings-attached affairs, you can't let a little thing like the sight of a shirt get you all unglued."

"I am not unglued."

"There's only one other emotion that could put that much color in your cheeks. I know. I pulled this shirt on yesterday and it smelled so strongly of your cologne I had to wash it and take a cold shower."

"Will you please have the decency to change the subject?"

He positively smirked. "Go on home."

"I appreciate this. You understand it's just this once."

"I'm well aware of your stipulations. I'll drop Alex off when practice is over."

Before she could do anything more than gasp and sputter, he turned and broke into a trot, hailing her daughter across the baseball diamond.

With more concentration than he knew he possessed, Marco put Alex through her paces. As the practice session continued, her shyness began to evolve into a steady determination. Marco took advice from Jake and from Ron Peterson, another team coach and father, as he honed the eight-year-old's skill.

Alex's improvement was matched by his relaxation. He was never tongue-tied, but as the session progressed he found he could kid and encourage without feeling awkward. Children—other people's—were creatures he knew little about. At twenty-nine he had yet to decide whether he wanted his own.

Lindsey stayed on the hill, keeping it all under her watchful eye. After twenty minutes Alex grumbled, "My mom's like an eagle. She thinks she has to be everywhere I am. I wish she'd stopped watching."

"Makes you nervous?"

"She's all worried." She broke into a grin. "Besides, I want to go home in your car."

"You go in for the sporty models, huh?"

"Sure."

"Don't worry about your mom. She loves you a lot," Marco said. "Maybe because you lost your dad, she thinks she has to be both parents. It probably makes her want to keep you extra close." He stopped abruptly, suddenly horrified that he'd raised what might be a painful subject.

"Dad used to bring me, my first year, even when he lived at the Dorset. He was a good thrower, too. Mom doesn't need to worry. I told her to go home."

"So did I."

"Well, if you're her boss, then she better listen."

"I'm more like a partner."

"Well, she acts like you're a boss. She yelled at Justin for even asking who you were. You draw, right?"

"Right."

"I think she might be having a hard time with the work she's doing for you."

"More yelling?"

"Nah. She was crying in her office last night."

Marco's heart jumped. "Are you sure?"

"I heard her. I think she was having a hard time with your work."

"I'll talk to her about working too hard."

Alex suddenly waved at Lindsey's retreating car. "She's finally leaving. Great! I guess she doesn't hate you, after all."

"Hate me?"

Alex grimaced. "I didn't mean that. She was swearing at you while she was crying. She didn't know I heard." She kicked the dirt. "You won't tell her I told you that, will you? I'll be grounded for life."

"I promise."

"Good. Now can we go out for some fly balls?"

"Sure." He'd done his own share of swearing.

At five-thirty he packed an exhausted Alex into his car and drove her back to York Road. He thought about taking her to a fast-food restaurant on the way, but he'd suffered enough of the wrath of Lindsey Major Russell for a while. Instead he drove directly to the neighborhood and eased his car into their driveway.

"Thanks," Alex said as they stopped.

"You're a good player. We'll do it again."

"When?"

"When?" he repeated.

Her face fell. "Oh, I guess you were just being polite."

"No, I'd like to, but it's sort of up to your mother. She's the boss when it comes to things like this."

"Rats."

"How about if I come in and ask her?"

Alex shook her head. "You have to ask parents things at the right minute. Brooke might be giving her a hard time or something. I'll ask her when I know it's the best time. My next practice is Thursday."

As Marco laughed, Justin threw open the front screen door and streaked across the lawn. "This is an awesome car! I saw it from the bathroom window the day I stubbed my toe. Boy, did you drive Alex home?"

"Yes, and I can see that your toe must be better."

"Sure. You better get out of there, Alex."

"It's none of your business," she replied.

Justin leaned over and looked across Marco at her. "Does Mom know you got in a car with a practically stranger? She didn't even want it in the driveway last time."

Alex looked mortified. "You are totally rude. He's just jealous," she said anxiously to Marco.

"It's all right, Justin. Your mom knows," he replied, already overwhelmed by the simultaneous conversations, grumbling and explanations.

Lindsey hurried across the lawn, arrived at the car and put her hands on Justin's shoulders. "Thank you for bringing her home."

"Ow!" the boy said.

"See," Alex whispered, "you never know how things are going around here. Thanks, Marco," she added in a normal voice.

"Please call him Mr. D'Abruzzi."

"Mr. D'Abruzzi. Whatever."

Marco watched as Alex assessed the situation. She seemed suddenly coy with her mother. "You know, Mom, Mr. D'Abruzzi's an awesome fielder. You should see everything I learned. Coach Peterson thinks he should keep helping me."

"Does he?"

"Thursday. It's Coach Peterson's idea."

"Mr. D'Abruzzi's a busy man, Alex."

"Just say you'll think about it."

Alex grinned at him, but Lindsey sighed and offered an unreadable look as he put the car into reverse. "We'll let you know," she said to him.

"Give me a call."

He idled the engine, then decided there was no sense waiting for an invitation to stay. She'd never offer it. He left wishing he could have given Justin a ride, or gotten a definitive answer about the practice session on Thursday. He had two things he could offer these kids with the hole in their lives. He yawned as he turned at the corner, and decided the lack of invitations was just as well. He was tired, too, and already looking forward to the peace and quiet of Dorset Court.

The thought of Lindsey crying over him stayed with him for the night. Maybe she had been right, and the day would come when the sight of her wouldn't bring the flush, or the desire, but it hadn't yet. Not when one look told him how she still felt. Let her think he'd worn the shirt on purpose. Hell, he'd wear it every time they met if he thought it would continue to elicit such a passionate response in her. It was true that contentment had been shaken out of him, but his need for her ran just as deep as the night they'd kissed over the waterwheel.

Seventeen

On Monday a bout of unsettled weather arrived, and rain began falling steadily by noon. Lindsey snapped on her office light as she tried to work at home. Self-analysis, recalled conversation, regret, confusion all played havoc with her ability to concentrate. She was glad she'd been honest with Marco. He *was* overwhelming. Even the idea that she was involved with him was overwhelming. She wasted hours in reverie, and all the while a little voice kept adding "nevertheless, nevertheless ..."

The unraveling of life with Jonathan had forced her to live one day at a time. She hadn't been wrong in thinking Marco was what she needed—for now. There was no denying that while she'd kept her professional and family lives separate, the relationship with the handsome, irreverent creative director had become the self-prescribed cure for what ailed her. Selfish as it might have been, her private time with Marco had given her a fresh, invigorated outlook, a sense of excitement that brightened every other aspect of her life.

It was also undeniably true that she felt more alive, more creative, more attuned to life than she'd felt in months. All right, years. "Years and years," she whispered to the empty sun room.

It was time to recognize the fact that the man worked a magic she'd forgotten existed. The closer she got to him, the more she understood herself and her own needs. But the key to it all had slipped from the lock. The rest of her life was no longer separate. It didn't take much more soul-searching to conclude that the only way to maintain the separation was to be aggressive about it.

What was good for her was not necessarily good for three children in need of a father figure. She had no intention of including them in a relationship based on nothing more substantial than raging hormones. She might be a neophyte when it came to affairs, but she was astute enough to know that handsome, young, creative, impetuous art directors did not offer long-term security.

"Call the shots," she told herself as she listened to the rain hit the roof and sheet against the windows. She needed to talk, needed Marco to understand her need for boundaries. However, during the day, when she had the privacy to discuss it, Marco was at the office with Karen and clients. When Marco was home alone, she had three children to contend with. Nothing was going to be discussed, established or resolved at a baseball field or a business office, and no polished and professional copy was going to come from her brain until she had her priorities settled.

After she greeted her damp children at three o'clock, she hired a neighborhood teenager for the afternoon and early evening, and tried to work uninterrupted. At five-thirty Lindsey looked in on the group, all of whom were in the kitchen slicing carrots and chopping celery for dinner. She looked at her watch. Her heart began its all-too-familiar thumping as she went over Marco's phone number with the sitter.

"Why do you have to go see him again? Why can't he come here, and give me a ride?" Justin asked.

"That would be taking advantage of him."

"When are you coming home?"

"As soon as I can. We have some work to go over."

"We don't have baby-sitters for your other bosses."

Guilt raised a flush. "I know, Justin, I know. I'll try to be back to kiss you good-night."

Alex looked at her carrot. "When are you going to decide if he can coach me?"

"It's not a good idea," Lindsey replied as she pulled on her raincoat.

"He said he would."

"He's very busy, darling. Maybe he just didn't want to hurt your feelings. You mustn't put people on the spot."

Brooke scoffed at her sister. "Alex, he's Mom's boss. You don't ask bosses to play baseball with you, or drive you in their fancy car, Justin."

The eight-year-old scowled. "He told me he wanted to coach me. He wasn't being polite."

Lindsey arrived at Dorset Court under her umbrella, with their conversation still echoing in her head and her heart knocking against her ribs. Marco opened the door after the first ring. He had on loose jeans and a flowing cotton shirt rolled up along his forearms, a close facsimile to her own attire. There was a paintbrush tucked over his ear.

"Well, I'll be damned." He did nothing to hide his surprise, but his expression was still guarded. "Spontaneity is an irresistible trait in a woman."

"You're working."

"Come and see."

She followed him down the hall into the studio. It was fully lighted this time, for work. His drawing board had the energy-commission work pinned on it, and the dragon illustration lay on the table, completed and matted. They stood side by side and looked at it together. Marco was still.

"It's beautiful."

"One of the things we did perfectly together," he answered, without making any attempt to touch her. "As I worked on it, I couldn't help but think it must be somehow connected to your children. Now that I know you have children."

"We make up bedtime stories together. The shy dragon trying to be fierce is one of the favorites."

He nodded without replying.

She winced. "I came over hoping we could talk."

"Trouble with the assignment?"

"No. I'll have it ready by Thursday, I hope."

"What's left to discuss? I thought all other aspects of your life were off-limits."

Lindsey sighed. "I don't mean to be difficult. What I want is a simple life, without a lot of complications."

"The way we were before I made the big discovery."

"I don't expect you to understand—you're not a parent, you have no other intrusions in your life. But a little empathy would be nice."

"Intrusions. I suppose that's what I am, too."

"A welcome one. I loved what we had." She picked up an eraser. "This was a bad idea. I don't even know what I wanted to say."

"What did you want to hear?"

She shook her head. "That we could continue? That we have something worth maintaining?" When he didn't reply, she turned. "I should have called. You were obviously working and I'm interrupting."

Marco leaned back against the table. "You've been nothing but an interruption and distraction since the moment I laid eyes on you. Or you laid hands on me." He laughed softly. "Have you made a decision about my coaching Alex?"

"I think you know the answer."

"Lindsey, if I had even one answer where you were concerned, I'd be happy."

Lindsey paused. "She seems to think I'm in the heartbreaking business."

"You said I wouldn't coach her."

"Couldn't."

"Did you give her a reason?"

"Marco, don't you see what's happening?"

"Of course I see what's happening. I fouled up your grand scheme and showed up at your house to discover your secret life. I'm not asking to be a part of it. I'm not sure I'm even cut out for it, but there's no taking back the moment. It's done. Just don't make me out to be the bad guy with Alex."

"My children aren't your concern. You know how hard I tried to keep this from happening."

"It must have been exhausting."

The tension was as high as the humidity, and for a long moment the only sound was the rain on the window. "I think I'd better get back. My sitter's on a tight schedule." Lindsey turned and glanced at Marco. For a moment he looked as though he'd pull her into his arms. She ached for it.

"Suit yourself," he replied instead.

Lindsey was home by seven-thirty. At nine, with the house quiet, she finally gave in to her frustration and called Marco from her office phone.

"I'm interrupting?" she asked at the sound of his hello.

"Look, Lindsey—"

"Marco..." She paused and laughed. "I don't want to leave things on such a low note. I actually called to tell you that your illustration is wonderful. We got off on other things.... I don't think you realize how impressed I am, and how much it means."

"Teamwork."

"Your talent and creativity brought my simple idea to life."

"You were the inspiration."

"Thank you, Marco."

His voice was strained and his sigh was deep, but there was no anger in either. "I like what we do together, even when I don't agree with your philosophy."

"Which we won't discuss now or we'll be right back to fighting."

"True. Sleep well. You know where I want you."

"Good night, Marco."

Lindsey hung up and sat listening to the incessant rain, until a sixth sense made her turn. She opened the French doors that separated the sun room from the living room to find her daughter tiptoeing toward the staircase.

"Alexandra?"

"You never call me that unless I'm in big trouble."

Lindsey pointed to the couch and her daughter sat down. "What's going on? It's not like you to eavesdrop. You were all tucked in for the night."

"I couldn't sleep."

Lindsey softened and tried to hug her, but the child pulled away. "Is it Brian Hammel again?"

"Ryan. It's not me. It's you."

"Me?"

"You and Mr. D'Abruzzi. He made you cry last week. I thought that was why you won't let him coach me. I thought you didn't like working for him 'cause he was mean. But you keep getting baby-sitters and going over to his house, and you don't even look like yourself when he's around.''

Lindsey sat very still and gathered her thoughts. Then she urged Alex to her feet, and they walked upstairs together. "Darling, Marco and I do work together, and some of the projects are difficult. I do go and see him. We're also friends. It's complicated, because sometimes adults aren't any better at things than children.''

"Sometimes they're worse.''

Eighteen

Marco's week dragged, weighed down by an endless list of irritations, from the dull task of proofreading copy to the fact that his local supplier had to back-order illustration board, and a set of typeface was returned from the printer set in the wrong point. Amanda called, and it took every ounce of acting ability he possessed to rid his voice of frustration. He gave his advertising partner an honest appraisal of Lindsey's work, describing in detail her talent and sixth sense when it came to teamwork. He had to bite back the urge to add that the writer was the most complicated, provocative woman he'd ever become entangled with.

On Thursday he fought with Karen over the due date of a simple brochure and didn't get around to apologizing for his mood until he was getting a second cup of coffee. He stopped at her desk. "Not one of my better days," he said.

"Not one of your better weeks. You need Amanda back, or else you need Lindsey. It must be one or the other," she muttered as she accepted his apology.

"Lindsey who?"

Her scoffing noise made him grimace.

"Males are so transparent. Honestly, Marco, for a man who prides himself on his knowledge of women, you're clueless about the effect they have on you."

"I'm immune to all of them, especially the ones I work with."

"I don't believe that for a minute and neither do you." Karen turned her back on him and picked up the jangling phone.

As if to prove the point, Lindsey arrived at eleven-thirty. Marco listened to her greet Karen, and the sound of her voice went right up his spine. He was at the computer, shifting graphics around on the screen. The glance she gave him was wary, guarded.

"Coffee?" he asked.

"No, thanks."

"Sit down. I'll be with you in a minute."

Lindsey sat on the edge of her chair as Marco continued at the computer. She had on a green cotton sweater with the sleeves pushed back to the elbows, and yellow slacks. He could feel her disconcerting stare as he worked, but when he turned from the screen, she looked away. She handed him a professional-looking folder. She'd finished the entire task, right down to the final draft and the billing statement.

"I can leave this with you. Call me later when you've had a chance to look it over."

"Now's as good a time as any." She sat back stiffly and he leaned over as he read. Occasionally he nodded. It was excellent. "Perfect. Amanda will love it. I've been giving her updates. Makes her want to rush right back."

"I appreciate the flattery."

"Seriously. A month's a long time to be away, even though two weeks of her trip is business. She needs to hear that her instincts about you were sound." He cocked his head. "You don't look thrilled."

Lindsey sighed. "You know, two weeks ago I would have told you this would be a crowning moment for me. I would have guessed that I'd be nervous, or at least anxious."

"But now?"

"The anxiety comes from something else entirely."

Karen knocked on the open door. "I'm going to lunch. Remember the phones. You want anything?"

Lindsey shook her head, while Marco replied that he'd go out himself, later.

"You were mentioning anxiety," he repeated when Karen had left.

"I only meant that I'm not nervous about these assignments. We work well together. I want to make sure we continue the relationship."

"We work beautifully together. You're excellent. I don't intend to jeopardize it. I'll submit this part of your bill, but I want you to continue with the energy project. Maybe on a retainer basis. You and Amanda can negotiate it when she gets back. Think about a reasonable fee."

"I'm always reasonable," she replied as she stood up.

Marco grinned for the first time and shook his head. He got to his feet as well and walked with her to his office door. "Reasonable is not an adjective that comes to mind when describing you."

"What adjectives do?"

He paused. His smile was molasses, slow and terse. "Sharp, talented, organized, educated . . ."

"Please continue."

"Darling, voluptuous, tantalizing, frustrating . . ."

The humor diffused the tension. The air between them crackled with unspoken anticipation. The anxiety she'd referred to began to jab up under his ribs. He remained uncharacteristically quiet and studied her.

"Don't look at me that way," she whispered. "You make it hard to think."

"Think? I can't think. All I can do is remember, and ache all over again. You're the most spontaneous woman I've ever met, yet you've got this damned air of mystery, this ironclad resolve that hounds me. I don't know what the hell to say, let alone *think.*"

She leaned back against the wall and sighed. "How about a sort of truce? The opera people gave me tickets to *La Boheme* for tomorrow night. Would you like to go?"

He put his hands on the wall, on either side of her head, and looked into her eyes, really looked. "Yes," he said.

Marco was so close her breasts brushed his chest. She leaned forward, nearly kissing him as she murmured, "I've missed this."

Her breath tickled his mouth and he filled his lungs with the scent of her cologne. "Have you?" The fabric of her shirt rustled against his, and beneath, her softness teased him unmercifully. "Have you?" He closed his eyes, only to be assaulted by the vision and memory of Lindsey naked in the doorway of his bedroom, cupping the light in her hands.

He slid his own hands over her, feeling the instant physical response he ached for, and played with her hair. Even with his jaw clenched, a moan rose in his throat. "Ah, Lindsey. You do have an irresistible streak. I want as much of you as I can get. I swear I could make love to you right here, standing up."

"Heaven knows you're trying." She wiggled sideways, making obvious attempts at smoothing out her breathing. "Wait until tomorrow." She moved further. "This relationship is based on work."

"Kiss me. That's the best base of all." He leaned her against the wall again and kissed her hard, deeply, until she panted softly against him. Marco let the sensations weave through him from scalp to toe. This woman brought him to life the way no one else ever had. When he finally caught his breath, he looked at her. "Friday night. I have a few conditions."

"No demands that I spend the night?"

"They were never demands."

"You see now that I have three perfectly legitimate reasons for turning you down."

"I would have seen *then* if you'd been honest."

"You do understand."

"Spending the night, yes. The rest of it, no. No, I don't." He swayed against her, his words whispered pressure against her mouth. "I don't understand. Tomorrow night I'm going to pick you up and take you home."

"That isn't necessary."

"I'll be the judge of what's necessary. It's what I need from you and it's not too much to ask. We're friends and we're business associates. Neither of those relationships will affect your children just because I'll be seen at your door."

"Marco, Alex has already questioned me. She's overheard a few phone conversations and she's confused. I don't—"

"Then for heaven's sake, think about it, Lindsey. It's in your best interest for your kids to see you as a three-dimensional person. You work, you play, you have men associates and friends. So do they. What they don't need is a mother who sneaks out of the house for clandestine—"

"You're making me sound terrible."

"I'm not going to loom out there on the horizon as some mysterious guy who takes their mother away. I know how you think. You probably don't give them any explanations, just baby-sitters. So take it or leave it. I'll be by about six-thirty. That'll give us time before the show to grab a quiet dinner near the opera house or, if you're so inclined, a quick trip back to my place for some fabulous lovemaking. Your choice." He smiled at the flash and turmoil in her eyes. "I'll even dress the part."

"Anything else?"

"Plenty, but the rest can wait. It'll give us something to discuss, since I'll be tired of business, and the rest of your life is off-limits to me. As my mother would say, *Così.*"

"*Così.* Please translate."

He finished with a decidedly Italian gesture that combined a shrug and a nod. "So. It's decided."

Lindsey's maternal concern replaced her grin as she opened her front door at six twenty-five Friday evening. Justin, who'd been down the street with a group of friends, came flying into the driveway on his bike and was now hanging on Marco's every word as the two of them looked over his car.

As she watched, they turned and walked to the house together, Justin all grass stains and smudges from head to toe, Marco looking like Madison Avenue's idea of an upscale Saturday-night escort. Marco's flare with clothes and the way they fit him set him apart whether he was standing on a baseball field or in the midst of hundreds of Wilmington's music patrons. His dark designer suit was complemented by a pale blue shirt and familiar tie. His dark eyes, framed by thick lashes, sparkled.

Lindsey stood at the door in the emerald green dress she'd worn to the mill and smiled as recognition changed Marco's expression.

"Look who's here, Mom!"

"Hello, Marco."

"What a great surprise, huh, Mom?"

Marco looked from the boy to his mother. "You haven't mentioned me?"

"Justin, Jill's in the kitchen with your sisters." She turned to Marco. "Obviously they know I'm going out."

"You just neglected a few details."

Alex, Brooke and their sitter appeared behind her. Alex gave them both full scrutiny. "Well, I guess you guys aren't going to work."

Marco jammed his hands into his pockets. "I was in the neighborhood and thought your mother might like to take in an opera."

"Opera? Yuk. Stay here instead." Justin turned to his mother. "Then I can have a ride. Please let me ask him."

"No, darling. Now scoot."

Justin looked from one to the other. "You're all dressed up. Is this like a date?"

Brooke jabbed him. "Don't be a dork. Mom doesn't date."

Lindsey smiled. "Actually, I'm taking Marco to the opera. We're just using his car."

The final comment came from Jill. "Mrs. Russell, did you say they could have the ice cream after dinner?"

"After dinner and after baths." She kissed Justin and went over last-minute instructions, then finally followed Marco to the car. The second she slid into the seat, she leaned her head back. "That wasn't the reception I would have planned."

"Dressed to the nines and you still didn't tell them I was going to pick you up. Maybe you should have walked down the block and met me by a tree."

"Don't belabor the point."

"I won't risk ruining the evening. It's the 'Mrs. Russell' that threw me. I still can't get used to it. Frankly, I don't know how you do it. Not that they're not great kids. It just looks so exhausting."

"The rewards are endless," she replied too quickly.

"I'm sure they are."

"I can do without the sarcasm."

"It wasn't sarcasm. I was only making conversation about something I know nothing about, and something you're not about to discuss. It's a little early for snapping my head off." He turned as he started the car. "Especially in *that* dress, from *that* night."

"And what night would that be?"

"I'd have thought you'd remember what you wore on such a significant evening. Of course, during the significant part, you weren't wearing it. May I suggest that we go directly back to Dorset Court and remove it again?"

"Dinner, D'Abruzzi."

"Yet another appetite to satisfy."

Nineteen

They settled on a small French restaurant at the city limits, and were shown to a secluded table. Memory startled Marco as he seated her, sliding his hand along the sleeve of her dress as he did. Their first time. Unwelcome images flooded him. The feel of her dress as they'd danced, the silkiness under his palms as he'd kissed her, the softness of her overheated skin beneath were as vivid as Lindsey herself. He felt the warmth in his cheeks as the images edged him toward arousal.

Lindsey was squinting, however, fighting pain in her head and back. "Too much gardening this afternoon," she replied to Marco's concern. "Too much guilt."

"Guilt?"

She sipped her aperitif. "There's no use pretending this relationship has been as easy as I thought it would be."

"You're not the type to separate your life into compartments, no matter what you'd have me believe. You're a fabulous woman, Lindsey, but you lack one major element that would ease headaches. Backaches, too, for all I know."

"Is this really the time for a lecture?"

"I never would have brought it up if I hadn't had those few moments with your kids when I picked you up. Why is it I can see what you can't?"

"My children—"

"Your children want some answers. They want to be able to trust me."

"Marco!"

"They're confused. Who the heck am I to you? They want answers, and if they don't get them, they'll make them up to suit. I want you to trust me, so they will."

"Trust you to do what?"

"For starters, trust me to coach Alex a couple of times a week without threatening our relationship or her stability. You can't give her a decent reason for not letting her have me as a coach, which means she can't understand why I won't be there for her."

"I told her you had a conflict."

"Then you lied."

"Marco!"

"I'm serious about this, Lindsey. I want you more than I've ever wanted a woman in my life, but I'm not going to be the wedge between you and Alex."

"Don't you see what's happening?"

"What I see is a disappointed little girl who's getting a raw deal for no reason. All she knows is that the guy her mother works for won't toss a ball a few times a week. I meant what I said the other night. I won't let you make me the bad guy in this. You're sure as hell not going to lie to her on my behalf. I've felt the brunt of your deception. It hurts."

Lindsey rubbed her temple and picked at her salad. Tears stung her eyes and she swore softly.

"Don't cry. I just want to get you to think about it."

"In theory, it all seemed so perfect. I've tried to keep you away because, frankly, I was doing what I don't want any of them to do—sneak around, fib. *Clandestine* was exactly the right word."

"Don't be so hard on yourself."

"Sex outside of any kind of commitment . . . I'm ashamed of myself."

"Lindsey, we're not reckless teenagers. We take precautions. Neither of us has any—"

She squeezed his arm. "Please remember where we are."

"As opposed to where we wish we were? You're implying this is some kind of spur-of-the-moment, high-risk behavior. You can distance yourself from me, but I don't know how you'll pull away from yourself. Maybe this is the time to ask ourselves exactly what it is we do want from this relationship. You've seemed completely satisfied with the status quo, insistent on it, in fact."

"It's all happened so fast, I've barely had time to think."

"I'm not sure analyzing it will do much good." Concern made him frown as she bit her lip. "Are you all right?"

"We need to talk about this."

"Fine, but you look like you're in pain. Is it worse?"

She squeezed his arm again. "I really thought I'd strained my back, but the pain's awful." A thin line of perspiration broke out on her upper lip.

Marco helped her to her feet. "Let me take you home."

She nodded. "I think you'd better. I'm sorry." In the time it took to explain to the waiter, her grip became a vise and her voice came between gritted teeth. "I need more than home. Can you get me to the hospital? I had one of these attacks when I was pregnant with the twins. There's nothing else like it in the world."

"Lindsey! Are you pregnant? Is this a miscarriage?"

She shook her head. "Kidney stone."

Marco pulled into the York Road driveway at ten-thirty that night and sat for one long moment with his head on the steering wheel. Contending with Lindsey Major, recalcitrant, feisty, creative copywriter was nothing compared to contending with Lindsey Russell, ailing mother of three. He'd stayed by her side through admissions, fished through her wallet for information on her medical coverage. Her grip nearly broke the bones in his hand, and her pain had torn him apart. Through it all she'd continued to bark instructions, insisting that he write them down. In his pocket was a torn piece of paper with barely coherent chicken scratchings:

Jill Crenshaw
Betsy O'Hare
seat belts
Justin—vitamins
Alex—baseball game 1 p.m. Sat.
cookies for Brooke's Brownie cookout

He didn't doubt for a minute that she would have added half-a-dozen other items, except that the pain medication knocked her out. He'd stayed long enough to speak with the emergency-room physician, whose prognosis was simple. Lindsey would be admitted and would stay until the stone was passed. They'd run some tests, followed by a urology workup when she felt better. Marco left the hospital with her green dress over his arm and her leather sandals in his hand.

Now he looked at the house. A lamp illuminated the front door and light shone from the living room. There was a dimmer glow through the glass of the back door, where he'd first gone in and taken biscuits out of the oven, where Alex had first demanded to know who he was and Justin's wail had drifted down from the bathroom. York Road and a little house that claimed far more of her life than he did...

Love for Lindsey Major Russell swept through him, as deep and intense as arousal.

* * *

Marco awoke with a start and a pumping heart. Sleep had eluded him for hours, but it had finally come, and now he opened his eyes, completely disoriented. A blur of small forms focused into Alex, Justin and Brooke. They were standing stone-faced at the foot of their mother's bed, staring at him.

"Hi." He sat up, bringing the comforter with him.

"Where's our mom?" Justin demanded.

"Where's Jill?" asked his twin.

Alex simply held up the green dress, her face ashen.

Marco rubbed his hair and his eyes as he chose his words. "Your mom is fine. She's had a kidney-stone attack and she's in the hospital."

Brooke's lower lip began to tremble.

"Kids, really, she's fine. We'll go see her." He explained as simply and calmly as possible, in terms he thought they'd understand, about what had happened and how she was feeling. It must have worked, because Brooke's lip returned to normal. "Last night after I made sure your mom was okay, I came to tell Jill and see if she could take care of you for a few days."

Brooke's lip began to tremble again. "The Crenshaws are going to Virginia today. She told us."

Marco nodded. "She told me, too. So you're in luck. You got me instead." No one looked particularly pleased. "Justin, I really wanted to sleep in that bunk bed of yours, but I was afraid I'd scare you in the middle of the night. When I was your age, I always wanted one. Never did get it, though."

"Grown-ups always tell stories about when they were kids," Alex murmured to Brooke, as if the comment needed justification.

Fatigue continued to press on him, but he gave them his most reassuring grin. "What's on the schedule when you guys get up?"

"We are up."

"Well, sort of. Let's see what time it is." He glanced at Lindsey's clock, bleary-eyed. "Six-fifteen. I don't suppose any of you would like to go back to sleep for a few more hours? No. Well then, some clothes would be next. Let's get dressed."

"We eat in our pajamas on Saturdays."

"In front of cartoons."

Marco nodded and fought the first wave of anxiety. "Since this isn't an ordinary Saturday, you guys are going to have something besides an ordinary breakfast."

"Where?"

"Why, Casa D'Abruzzi, of course. We'll have to get there in my car and probably put the top down, too."

"Awesome," Justin screeched. Then his face suddenly fell.

"I know what you're thinking. But your mom won't mind under these circumstances."

"Promise?"

"We'll call her in a while." There was too much at risk not to.

Marco sent the three of them to get dressed, and took the moment to slide back into the pillows. He looked at the pastel walls, the photographs, the novel on the bedside table. Lindsey's room, Lindsey's belongings, Lindsey's life. Other life. He closed his eyes and filled his lungs with the intimacy of it. Circumstances had plunged him into the midst of everything she'd wanted separate, and there was nothing in his experience that gave him the least sense that he might be capable of keeping chaos at bay. Anxiety made his palms sweat.

He got back into his dress shirt, suit pants, socks and Italian loafers, and found the children dressed and in front of the television set. At seven-fifteen, he got through to the nurses' station closest to Lindsey's room, where it was confirmed that she was awake, if uncomfortable. Marco was transferred to a sedated voice. "This isn't Jill," he tried for openers, in a cheerful voice. After the full explanation, Lindsey replied that he should have tried Betsy.

"Yell at me when you're healthy and home. There was no reason why I couldn't fill in. I've even been known to bake cookies, under duress."

"Marco, I don't want you there," she replied woozily. "You'll never cope. They'll run you ragged."

"Or they might like me. That's your biggest fear."

"Call Betsy."

"The little group will be fine. *We'll* be fine. To tell the truth, I like you like this. You're too groggy to put up an argument."

"Give me Alex," she murmured.

Marco leaned against the couch and watched as each child had a turn on the phone. The pinched anxiety in their faces lessened.

Nevertheless, reality and responsibility soon washed over him. He stripped Lindsey's bed, and had Brooke help him put fresh sheets on it while she explained that a slice-and-bake cookie dough was already in the refrigerator. He grabbed it and the kids, and eased his sports car from Lindsey's driveway. Everything she held dear in the world was seat-belted firmly in his passenger seats. "Who's ready for adventure?"

They looked back at his unshaven face silently.

He drove to Dorset Mills well under the speed limit as they held their faces to the wind. Oblivious as the children were, Marco stopped at each traffic light aware that he was unshaven, unbrushed and wearing his suit from the night before.

As he parked in his usual spot and turned off the ignition, Justin pulled himself up from the back seat. "Hey! This is where Dad used to live." The girls were silent.

"I forgot. Look, if you can just wait a minute, I'll grab my things and we'll go back to your house."

"I want to see *your* house."

"I don't think—"

"It's okay," Alex said. "Really."

In the privacy of the bathroom connected to his bedroom, Marco stood in his tartan boxer shorts and stared at his lathered reflection. So far the morning had been a series of hurdles, and he'd made it over every one—not necessarily gracefully, but he was still on his feet. "Not bad," he muttered as the door suddenly swung open.

"Hey, sport," he said to Justin, who stood looking up at him.

"Brooke wants another grapefruit."

"Tell her to help herself. They're all sliced."

By the time he'd pulled his razor from the drawer, the boy was back. "You shaving?"

"Yup."

"Mom shaves her legs."

"Women do that." Marco bent down. "Is it tough living with all those females?"

"Sometimes."

"I had *three* sisters and a mom. One bathroom, too."

"Jeepers." The boy took a step closer. "Did you have a dad?"

"I did. Still do. He's a great guy."

"My dad used to let me shave with him when I stayed over."

Anxiety stabbed again. "I bet you miss it."

Justin nodded. "We used to do a lot of neat things when I stayed over."

"Maybe we could do some neat things, too, while we wait for your mom to get well."

Justin was quiet, his voice suddenly small. "Is she really coming home?"

Marco went down on one knee and put his arms on Justin's thin shoulders. "Yes, just as soon as she can. She hurts, Jus, but she'll be fine."

The child blinked.

"I would never lie to you. We'll go and see her, if we can, and we'll bring her home when she's ready."

The six-year-old hastily brushed his eyes with the sleeve of his shirt while Marco slid open the drawer of the vanity and found an old razor. He removed the blade, opened Justin's small hand and gave him a healthy squirt of shaving cream. He brought a chair in from the bedroom and lifted him onto it.

"Lather up, buddy. I could use a little company."

"Really?"

"Really." They stood side by side in front of the mirror. Marco lifted his chin and stretched his jaw in his unconscious routine as he pulled the razor through the foam. Beside him the boy mimicked every gesture, right down to the slap of after-shave lotion on his clean cheeks.

"Women like us when we smell good," Marco added as he put the cap back on the bottle.

Justin jumped off the chair and headed for the door, where he paused. "Mr. Bruzzi, do you think you'd ever want to smell good for my mom?"

Marco winked at him. "It's Marco. Go have another sticky bun."

As Justin left, Marco stripped and got into the shower. He raised his face to the spray and pressed his balled fists against his eyes in a futile effort to hold back the emotions that continued to tear at him.

Twenty

Once Marco had pulled on fresh clothes, he greeted his restless group in his living room. "I need a cookie maker, and I thought you guys might like to see my studio."

Alex tapped him on the elbow as he led them into his work space. "If you're in charge of us all day, does that mean you can coach me in baseball before my game?"

"Yes, as soon as we finish the baking for Brooke."

"You're not too busy? Mom said—"

"She was afraid I wouldn't want to." He knelt. "I do want to, and I have time."

Alex nodded silently and picked up his illustration. She looked at it wide-eyed. "This is our story about the dragon. She used to tell it to us all the time. We'd help with parts."

"She told me about it, too. We worked on it together."

"You're an awesome artist. You guys could make it into a book. You'd be famous," Brooke added.

He laughed and showed them his equipment, from his light box to his gesso for preparing canvas. When he reached his desk, he pulled a sheaf of paper out of a drawer. "Can anybody think of someone who might like a homemade get-well card?"

They drew with childish determination that continued to heat his heart. His chest was full, which lessened his anxiety to manageable proportions. Marco left them long enough to clean up the dishes, lay out cookie sheets and preheat the oven. He also spent long moments staring out the window over the sink.

"Mr. Bruzzi?"

He turned around. "Wouldn't it be easier to call me Marco, buddy?"

Justin nodded. "Could you draw me a dragon, one I could keep in my room?"

"Sure, but I might need a little help."

The boy's grin split his face. "I'm good with crayons."

Another call to the hospital set the schedule for the afternoon. Lindsey had passed the kidney stone, but was undergoing a battery of tests that would take her through visiting hours. Nevertheless, if all went well, she could be discharged by dinnertime. Dinnertime. That morning the day had loomed like a bottomless well he'd been assigned to fill. Now he wasn't sure he'd have enough hours to accomplish everything he had in mind.

He and Brooke, who worked with barely a word, baked her batch of cookies, putting aside enough for dessert at lunch. In the next forty-five minutes the children finished their cards and colored in a welcome-home banner Marco had run off on his computer. They packed up the cookies, and the minute he locked the door behind them, Justin made a dash for the car.

"I call the front seat this time," Brooke yelled after him.

"No way. Boys up front. Girls in the back."

Marco put a canvas bag with the paraphernalia, a sweater and his baseball glove in the trunk while they scrambled into their seats. "We've got enough driving to do so that you can each get a chance, wherever you want to sit. Boys in the front to York Road." He winked at Justin and looked over his shoulder. "Brooke in the front to Alex's game. Alex in the front on the way home."

"That'll be twice for Alex."

Marco paused and turned on the ignition. "She's the oldest, and since she's the baseball star, she'll deserve it." He pulled a Baltimore Orioles' cap from his back pocket and put it on as he sat behind the steering wheel. "Got to have my lucky cap if I'm going to coach Alex this afternoon." The eight-year-old grinned at him in the rearview mirror.

"And Mom gets the front seat when we bring her home."

"She'll be our guest of honor," Marco replied, turning the car toward York Road.

The afternoon was comfortably warm, with occasional puffs of cloud drifting past the May sun. The perfect day for a picnic, he'd told them, amazed at their enthusiastic reaction when he suggested they pick up an order for four from Chicken For Supper on the way to the Little League field.

They chose the spot on the hill where he'd found Lindsey during his first jaunt to Myer's Field. It seemed weeks ago, a lifetime ago, since the three tousle-haired urchins had been unknown entities. He watched them eat, listened to their chatter. All self-consciousness had evaporated hours earlier, along with his anxiety. He was invigorated, constantly amazed and not a little proud of the way the day had progressed.

"We better practice," Alex said as they cleaned up the scraps.

Marco agreed and gave Brooke and Justin instructions to stay on the playground equipment or in plain sight. He showed them precisely where he and Alex would be, behind the bench on the east side of the field.

"I'll check on you every few minutes," he added. "Green shirt," he said as he tapped Justin's head. "Blue jacket." He tapped Brooke's.

"Mom never worries."

"Go only where she lets you." He fought the urge to tell them that he was certain she'd done little else but worry, alone in that sterile hospital room, hallucinating about Mendenhall and Lipton's creative director loose with her children. "I'm a little newer at this than she is. Humor me."

"What's that mean?" Justin demanded.

Marco leaned over and growled, "Do what I say!" which only produced giggles and twin dashes for the swings. Once they'd settled with the other children, he turned his attention to Alex, beginning with fly balls. He watched her scamper. Her uniform was red, with Brookfield Motors stitched on the back, framing her number, 7. He'd have to mention the idea of M & L sponsoring a Little League team to Amanda.

Marco tossed another ball and wondered just how much he'd have to mention to Amanda—how much of this completely unplanned adventure would be obvious to his business partner once she was back in the office Monday morning, putting in her usual nine-hour day. *Adventure.* He caught the returned ball. The word didn't begin to describe the emotional roller coaster he'd been hitched to since the weekend she'd left.

He sent Alex out for grounders and bounced one along the grass. He spotted the twins. Green shirt, blue jacket, he reminded himself. Brooke was on top of the slide, Justin on the tires. After another ten minutes, the regular coach called the team together for batting practice. Alex started for the batter's box, then stopped. "Thanks," she called. "You're really awesome."

"So are you, kid," he shot back.

Green shirt, blue jacket. He turned again to check on the twins before collapsing on their hillside blanket. Blue jacket. Brooke was now with two girls behind a tipped-over picnic table. Green shirt, green shirt... He spotted the blond boy on the slide. It wasn't Justin. Marco shot to his feet. Same shirt, different child. His heart lurched. Had he been watching the wrong kid all this time? Surely Brooke would have noticed. He sat back down and cleared his head as he scanned the crowd of children. The playground was a sea of activity, making it nearly impossible to keep track of one little form.

He reached Brooke as the game started and was introduced to the Harringtons, parents of her playmates in nearby lawn chairs watching the game. He forced his voice to normalcy. "Have you seen your brother?"

Brooke's glance grew confused when she came out from behind the table. She couldn't spot him among the children. "Maybe inside the tires." They walked together among the equipment, calling and asking and coming up empty.

Panic rose in Marco's chest as he wrestled with the sure knowledge that of course Justin was fine. Of course. He scanned the playground, the ball diamond, Alex on the bench with her teammates. He sent Brooke back to her friends, made her promise to stay put, and walked into the wooded area that bordered the playground. The other boundaries were the parking lot and the street, both of which were clearly visible. No green shirt. The woods weren't deep. He could see through the foliage to the backs of houses. What he couldn't see, or hear, was any sign of the six-year-old who'd tugged at his heartstrings since dawn.

"Justin?"

Nothing greeted him but the whisper of leaves and the distant shouts of the players and their fans.

"Justin?"

Ten minutes later Marco emerged, having walked along the property lines and back. He tried to think like a six-year-old. He tried to think like the mother of a six-year-old. What would Lindsey do? He came out of the woods at a trot and asked Brooke, in his least intimidating voice, to stay with the Harringtons for a few minutes, explaining the situation. He jogged to his car, intending to drive along the nearby streets.

The pain of concern and foreboding was worse than any anxiety, worse than the anguish he'd felt for Lindsey the night before. He focused on the line of cars dead ahead and spotted his, parked between a pickup truck and a station wagon. Sun bounced off the hood, and he was within ten feet of the front bumper when a flash of blond hair caught the light.

"Justin!" Marco reached the convertible as the youngster straightened up in the back seat and blinked. "What in the name of— Get out of there!"

The boy stood up, pale and frantic as he climbed over the side of the car and slid to his knees next to the station wagon. Marco reached him as his expression crumbled into fear and then he broke into great, gulping sobs. "I didn't break anything."

"You scared me to death. What are you doing over here? I told you to stay where I could see you. I've been in the woods. I told you..." Marco finally collapsed under the weight of his own fear and the terror he'd obviously struck in Justin.

"I got cold. I came over for my jacket," the child said in barely a whisper. "I couldn't find Brooke or you anywhere. You were lost. You weren't anywhere." Sobs choked him. "You weren't! I didn't touch anything! I just got in the back seat for my jacket. I just sat in your car. Not for long."

"I was in the woods looking for you." Marco couldn't think of anything else to say. Instead he pulled him up in a bear hug and sat him on the hood of the car. "Looking for you."

Justin leaned forward and buried his face in Marco's chest.

Twenty-One

Lindsey heard them before she saw them. The familiar lilting voices rose and fell as her children chattered their way down the hall from the elevator.

"I bet she's asleep."

"Don't be a dork. She's waiting for us."

"But she's real sick."

"Not anymore. Marco says the stone passed, remember."

"Do you think they'll let her keep it in a jar?"

"You can barely see it. Remember Marco's picture? A teeny dot."

"Marco says to be quiet. You'll wreck the surprise."

Lindsey sat on the edge of her bed and bit her lip at the "Marco, Marco, Marco" on each child's lips. The separation, the fragile balance she'd worked so hard to maintain between the people most dear to her had obviously evaporated. She grinned at the cacophony she loved, but held her breath at the implications.

"Okay, guys, this is it. Now remember what you practiced."

This voice, baritone, faint Boston accent, hushed and familiar, set her pulse racing, despite everything.

"Surprise!" They whispered it in unison and crowded in the door.

Lindsey put her hands to her cheeks in mock surprise. "My goodness. You're clean. You sparkle. Whose children are you?"

"Yours, Mom," Brooke replied.

"No game today? No playground?"

"Great game, Mom—we won by a mile. I caught the highest fly ball you ever saw, with two guys on base!" Alex handed her their cards.

Justin thrust his bunch of spring flowers wrapped in florist paper at her. "Marco made us take showers and get all cleaned up, that's all. We made the cards," he added. "Marco showed us how. He bought the flowers downstairs. He said girls like that stuff. He let us draw in his studio. He's really a good draw-er."

"I know, darling."

"We made my cookies, and ate some at lunch."

"We brought you clothes," Alex added. "Marco was all nervous about going through your stuff, so I picked out everything. I knew what to get."

Lindsey opened her arms and pulled her children close, then looked over their heads at Marco with tears in her eyes. "I've missed you guys."

"We've missed you. *They've* missed you," he added rapidly.

"There's more surprises at home," Justin added.

"Not if you give everything away," Alex replied.

Once Lindsey dressed—in the jeans and a favorite sweater, presented in a paper bag along with sneakers—she was discharged, tucked into the front seat of the car and peppered with questions. Yes, she'd passed the stone. Yes, it hurt, a lot. Yes, the medication made her feel better, and yes, she was tired, but totally, completely fine.

She had the usual instructions to increase her water intake and make an appointment with a urologist for a follow-up. She was given a prescription for pain medication in case she suffered another attack, all of which she explained in her best reassuring tone.

She leaned back against the headrest and answered their questions, listened to the description of the ball game and a convoluted tale about Justin going for a sweater and getting lost in the back seat of Marco's car. Through it all, Marco drove, commented and teased. It seemed oddly, dangerously natural.

They reached York Road at dusk, and it was then that she realized she had no idea what the next step was. Goodbye at the curb? See you Monday at the office? Stay for dinner before you go? Her children continued to monopolize the conversation until they were in the driveway.

"You'll never guess what we had for lunch. Chicken For Supper. Marco buys it all the time. His favorite is extra crispy, too! And you won't guess what we're having for dinner. Marco makes the same sweet-and-sour sauce as you, Mom. We're going to stir-fry. I'm helping,'' Justin said.

"I thought I'd stay till they're settled for the night. I thought you could use a hand," Marco added softly as the children barreled into the house, flicking on lights as they went.

Lindsey paused at the back-door stoop. "I don't know. I'm not sure it's a good idea."

Even in the dusk, the pain in his expression was clear. His dark lashes swept over a penetrating glance. "To your way of thinking, the damage is done, Lindsey. The boundary's been crossed. I'm sorry your sitter was unavailable, but she was. Your kids had me today. All day. I did my best to remain aloof, rude and thoroughly despicable, just to keep that all-important separation as strong as ever. They're probably dying for me to leave."

"Marco, I didn't mean—"

"I know exactly what you meant. It's nearly seven, your kids are starving. Come in and have some dinner with us—with them. You can argue with me later."

"I don't want to argue."

He leaned over. "Then for once in your life, do as you're told, before I kiss you speechless in front of all three of them."

The house smelled deliciously of Marco's recipe. Dinner was served by all of them, a parade of diminutive loved ones scurrying from kitchen to table with fried rice, green beans, snow peas and bits of beef sautéed in the sweet-and-sour sauce. The dining room table had been set, right down to Alex's centerpiece of greens and flowers from the backyard perennial beds. Welcome Home, Mom was strung in computer paper across the living room wall.

Conversation still centered on their day with Marco. Lindsey listened to it all, painfully aware that they seemed completely at ease with him.

At eight-thirty the four of them ganged up on Lindsey once again, and ushered her up to her bedroom. The sheets and towels were clean; more fresh flowers were on her nightstand. She stayed in her clothes, but lounged on the bed, where they served her dessert with a steaming cup of herbal tea. She drank it listening to the downstairs noises of dishes and silverware clinking, as Marco put them through the task of cleaning up. When they appeared again, all three children were dressed for bed.

Lindsey followed the girls into their room, tucked them in, listened to good-night prayers and kissed them both. Alex turned on her side. "Are you mad that Marco coached me today? He taught me a lot. He's not mean, if that's what you were afraid of. He's really nice, and he said he had time to do it again."

"I'm not mad. I'm very thankful he was able to help."

"Does that mean he can help again?"

"We'll see."

"I hate it when grown-ups say that. It always means no."

"It means we'll see. Good night, darling."

Justin was on his step stool examining his teeth in the bathroom mirror. "They're about as clean as they're going to get, buddy," Marco said from his perch on the edge of the bathtub.

"Two down, one to go," Lindsey said as she watched.

"I shaved this morning," Justin stated as he examined his chin. "Marco let me use his razor, like Dad. We used smelly water."

"You mean Marco's after-shave lotion?"

"Sure." He hopped off the stool. "Do you think Marco smells good?"

Marco stood up. "Time to hit the hay, sport."

Lindsey sighed ruefully. "He smells just fine."

Justin looked back at him. "Girls like smelly water, right?"

She watched as her son put his hand in Marco's. "Can he sleep over? There's space in my room. He always wanted bunk beds. He could have mine tonight—the top, even."

Lindsey's cheeks burned. "I don't think so, darling. Besides, you know it's not polite to ask things like that in front of people."

"But he needs to sleep over to take care of us in case you have to go back to the hospital."

Marco looked at Lindsey over the child's head. "Come on, sport, I'll tuck you in. I'm as close as a phone call."

They flicked on the bedroom light and headed for the bunk. A hand-drawn dragon breathing fire and dropping scales was tacked to the bulletin board over the desk.

Twenty-two

When the last child's light was out, Marco followed Lindsey back down the stairs. He was bone tired, and the reality of what the past twenty-four hours had brought was beginning to hit home. "I will go. I think I should, but not before we talk."

"There's a lot to be said."

He walked with her to the living room, but stayed on his feet. "I never planned this, Lindsey. I never expected half of what happened today. I came over here for you, scared to death, if you want the truth—feeling completely inadequate. I don't know what the kids'll tell you when I'm not around, but I learned as much about myself as I did about them."

"They obviously did fine, and I thank you."

"I know you, Lindsey Major. I'm sure you sat in

that hospital bed all day and stewed over the situation."

"You're right. I spent hours thinking, thinking about how incredibly selfish I've been. This thing with you has been a wonderful fling, but I've behaved like some besotted twenty-year-old with no one to consider but herself." She lowered her voice even farther and leaned toward him. "I've quenched this thirst, or fire, or whatever it was that made me behave so recklessly. I want you as a friend, I want you as a business partner, but you can't be just an on-again, off-again part of my children's lives. They aren't ready for that."

"It happens all the time in situations like these."

"Not to my children. This was just one day, a day you can leave behind you—children you'll leave behind you. What if they begin to expect you every weekend, every baseball game? They don't deserve more heartache."

The kernel of truth burrowed into his heart and started an ache behind his breastbone that he tried to ignore. "I guess I should be flattered that you're torn between your devotion to your principles and your mad, passionate desire for me."

"I've come to terms with what we've been doing. There are far more important things in my life than—" she paused, as if groping for words to make the right comparison "—passionate temptation in a business office, for heaven's sake."

"What temptation?"

"You know very well what temptation. Sneaking off to Dorset Court wasn't enough. You nearly...right there in your office…standing up. Marco, I'm through with this hedonistic behavior.''

The sudden focus of her anguish—the memory of her body against his—forced his pulse to throb in places he didn't dare think about. The sudden heat drove a flush into his complexion. He knew better than to comment. Instead, he put his hands on either side of her face.

''Something that feels so right, that brings you and me such pleasure, has got to be rooted in more than hedonism.'' He kissed her lightly and stepped back. ''Lindsey, your kids and your conversation have worn me out. I'm going home, just the way you wanted. Amanda arrives tomorrow and it'll be business as usual on Monday. It would be nice if I made some sense when I talk to her. I meant what I said to Justin, though. I'm as close as the phone if you or the kids need me.''

''Thank you.'' Her eyes shone with the beginning of tears.

Although her mood would have been better served by a steady downpour, Sunday dawned clear and breezy. Lindsey kept to the usual routine of church for the four of them and lunch together afterward. The children played with neighborhood friends until four o'clock, then they all trooped to the Brownie cookout, cookies in hand. It was Brooke who commented that it didn't seem fair that Marco wasn't there, since he'd baked them.

The day ended with baths, stories and three exhausted children tumbling into bed. Justin was the last to settle, murmuring as she tucked him in that he'd wished he could have shaved with Marco again. *We wish a lot of things,* she answered silently as she kissed his tousled hair.

She got ready for bed herself, in a pink cotton nightshirt, treated herself to a glass of sherry and settled in front of the television, still unable to dismiss the one constant intrusion into an otherwise uninterrupted day.

The gentle knock at her front door startled her into a sitting position. When it came again she walked the short distance and snapped on the front light. Marco D'Abruzzi, as striking as the Sunday she'd first spotted him, was on her brick steps. He had on his usual khaki pants, with a loose blue chambray shirt open over a flamboyant Hawaiian one. *The* Hawaiian one. Her hands fluttered at her neck. She opened the door a crack.

His look was serious. "Is it too late for a house call? I knew you'd never come out to my place, and I waited till I thought the kids would be asleep."

"Marco, you shouldn't."

He pivoted. "Neighbors?"

"Neighbors have nothing to do with this."

"Pounding heart, racing pulse, sweaty palms?"

She opened the door wider. "For heaven's sake, stop it."

"I was talking about me." His voice fell away to a faint cough as he drank in the sight of her. "I was hoping we could talk."

"Haven't we said enough?"

"Not nearly enough. I tried to discuss the past three business weeks with Amanda this morning, who wanted to know how you were working out, of course. That was tough enough. Then I had a long, quiet, normal, Marco D'Abruzzi Sunday to think. My god, it was empty. I had to invent activities. Now I've come to talk."

"We did talk."

"No, *I'm* going to talk. You're going to listen." He put his hands on her shoulders. "You were right to worry yesterday. We bonded, as they say—the Little League player, the shy twin, the rambunctious bundle of energy and me. We had a good time, we weathered some scary moments. I handed out discipline when they needed it, and they corrected me when I was wrong. There was only one piece of the puzzle missing. You. Of course, you had to have been missing or none of it would have happened."

"You're no good with kids—you've said so."

"I was wrong. I'm not half-bad. With yours."

She winced. "You know how I feel. You can't fault me. Surely you see now how vulnerable they are."

"What I saw yesterday, what stayed with me through the night and brought me awake this morning, wasn't the thought of you, for once. It was them." Suddenly he pulled off his outer shirt and thrust it at her. "Could you put this on if you're going to stand there and breathe like that?"

She flushed and pulled it over her shoulders, and then glanced at the staircase, which ran right up from the small living room. "You'll wake the kids. If you're going to talk so personally, let's go to my office." She led him past the couch, through the French doors into the sun room and closed them behind her.

"I used to try to picture where you worked, where you went when you left me—the intriguing, independent, single woman without a care or responsibility...." He ran his hand over the sleeve of his shirt and up to her cheek. "The point I'm trying to make is that what I saw were three very different, distinct little people in need of some answers in their lives. They wanted more than just yesterday. I do, too. I want to do this again, the five of us. We ate well. We played hard. We laughed. I still need a good night's sleep, but I won't get one until this is settled. Running back to Dorset Mills as if nothing has changed was ludicrous."

"But we had everything worked out between us."

"We had nothing worked out between us that has anything to do with your real life. We haven't quenched any thirst, extinguished any fire. I want you as much as ever." Marco stroked her hair. "When I met you, you fit every fantasy I ever had about women. You made no demands, you asked nothing more of me than what you gave. Everything was perfect in the beginning, for both of us. I can't blame you for not wanting any responsibility, after what you've been through. But the fact is you are responsible and so am I, for each other and for those kids. Why the hell isn't life perfect now? Because you taught me some basic truths about myself. No one has ever touched me the way you do. You bring a need, an intensity that deepens every time you make love to me. I've thought that need came from some place I'd never reach, but I reached it, Lindsey. I found the place. I love you. I want to love all of you."

"Love?"

"The way you can love me, completely, totally."

"But what if it doesn't work? What if we make terrible decisions that affect them?"

"It's already working. You know it as well as I do, if you'll just open your eyes and that frightened heart of yours. What you're playing at isn't love. I've got your body, but I need your heart, and you need mine." He grinned. "I'm the best thing that's ever happened to you, and we can make this work. We can let three fatherless children see the balance that's created when a man and woman are committed to each other and to a future together."

"Love."

"Love. The starting-from-now-and-lasting-forever kind. The marry-me-and-live-happily-ever-after kind. It does exist. The kind that makes you want to wrap three little kids in your arms and keep them safe, give them balance. The kind that makes you want to make love to their mother—" he leaned and kissed her, hard, deeply, the way he always had "—standing up."

"Marco, it's a huge commitment," she murmured with her lips against his open mouth.

"I'm ready. I've been ready. It just took you—all of you—to make me realize it. You're ready, too, darling, if you'll just open your eyes and your heart."

"I love you, Marco. Alex, Brooke and Justin love you already, I think. That's what terrifies me."

"I won't let you down."

"I believe you."

He began to play over her cotton-covered breasts, panting softly in time with her. "Won't Amanda be—"

"Not a word to her yet. Not a word!"

"There you go again, handing out directives." He sighed.

"I've got another one." She leaned to the left and locked the door, then put her arms around his neck and whispered, "Standing up."

He chuckled and leaned to the right, snapping off the light. She grinned at the rustle of fabric as his khaki gabardine dropped to the floor, then gasped as he suddenly reached up under her nightshirt. Friction from hip to toe drove a heat into her that weakened her knees. She played with shirttails and fought for balance.

"I love you," he moaned until there were no words left.

She began the familiar finger-walk, but over uncharted territory.

"No puppet ever ventured there," he gasped.

"Che sorpresa," she whispered in return.

*   *   *   *   *

SILHOUETTE®

Desire®

MAN
of the
Month

1994

They're the hottest books around...with heroes you've grown to know—and *love*....

Created by top authors—the ones *you* say are your favorites....

Don't miss a single one of these handsome hunks—

MOM94JD

WOLFE WATCHING
by Joan Hohl

Undercover cop Eric Wolfe knew *everything* about divorcée
Tina Kranas, from her bra size to her bedtime—without ever
having spent the night with her! The lady was a suspect, and
Eric had to keep a close eye on her. But since his binoculars
were getting all steamed up from watching her, Eric knew it
was time to start wooing her....

WOLFE WATCHING, Book 2 of Joan Hohl's devilishly sexy
Big Bad Wolfe series, is coming your way in July...only
from Silhouette Desire.

IT'S OUR 1000TH SILHOUETTE ROMANCE, AND WE'RE CELEBRATING!

JOIN US FOR A SPECIAL COLLECTION OF LOVE STORIES BY AUTHORS YOU'VE LOVED FOR YEARS, AND NEW FAVORITES YOU'VE JUST DISCOVERED.
JOIN THE CELEBRATION...

April
REGAN'S PRIDE by Diana Palmer
MARRY ME AGAIN by Suzanne Carey

May
THE BEST IS YET TO BE by Tracy Sinclair
CAUTION: BABY AHEAD by Marie Ferrarella

June
THE BACHELOR PRINCE by Debbie Macomber
A ROGUE'S HEART by Laurie Paige

July
IMPROMPTU BRIDE by Annette Broadrick
THE FORGOTTEN HUSBAND by Elizabeth August

SILHOUETTE ROMANCE...VIBRANT, FUN AND EMOTIONALLY RICH! TAKE ANOTHER LOOK AT US! AND AS PART OF THE CELEBRATION, READERS CAN RECEIVE A FREE GIFT!

YOU'LL FALL IN LOVE ALL OVER AGAIN WITH SILHOUETTE ROMANCE!

Silhouette®

CEL1000

SILHOUETTE® Desire®

They're sexy, they're determined, they're trouble with a capital *T!*

Meet six of the steamiest, most stubborn heroes you'd ever want to know, and learn *everything* about them....

August's *Man of the Month,* Quinn Donovan, in
FUSION by Cait London

Mr. Bad Timing, Dan Kingman, in
DREAMS AND SCHEMES by Merline Lovelace

Mr. Marriage-phobic, Connor Devlin, in
WHAT ARE FRIENDS FOR? by Naomi Horton

Mr. Sensible, Lucas McCall, in **HOT PROPERTY**
by Rita Rainville

Mr. Know-it-all, Thomas Kane, in **NIGHTFIRE**
by Barbara McCauley

Mr. Macho, Jake Powers, in **LOVE POWER**
by Susan Carroll

Look for them on the covers so you can see just how handsome and irresistible they are!

Coming in August only from Silhouette Desire! CENTER